# The Perception Glitch

## & Yogic Code of Debugging the Mind

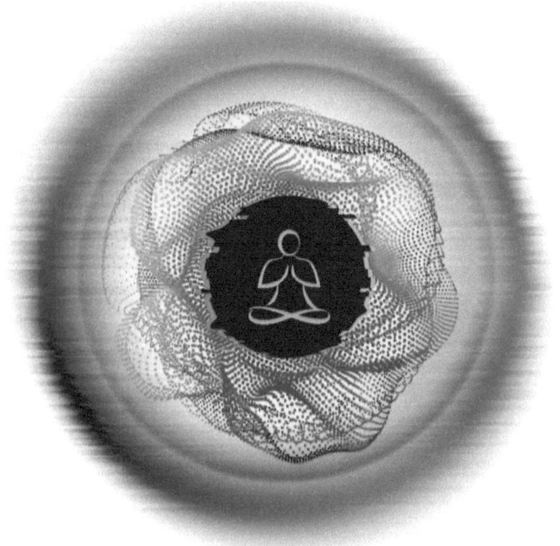

Vol.1: On Attainment

(Patañjali Yoga Sutras: Samādhi Pāda)

# Dr. Tejaswi Katravulapally

Copyright © 2025 Dr. Tejaswi Kataravulapally

All rights reserved

No part of this publication may be reproduced, distributed, or transmitted in any form or by any means, including photocopying, recording, or other electronic or mechanical methods, without the prior written permission of the author, except in the case of brief quotations embodied in critical reviews and certain other noncommercial uses permitted by copyright law.

*The book is dedicated to my revered Guru*

## Master. E. K.

*who is ever present in my heart!*

# Contents

# Preface

'Yoga-sūtras of Patañjali' is one of the foremost spiritual works that has received extensive commentary from the greatest stalwarts throughout the world. Why is it so revered? It seems that the instructions given are simple, yet profound, concise, yet exhaustive, logical and yet mystical. Thus, the world's masters at their destined time to turn world-events, expounded upon this masterpiece according to the language palatable to their era.

The advent of modern science, such as quantum technologies that delve into the atomic world and space technologies that explore the vastness of space, has had a profound impact on human attitudes. Even those who are not well-versed in modern science are now familiar with Albert Einstein and his theory of mass-energy equivalence. As a result, it is reasonable to conclude that the world is far more advanced than it was a few thousand years ago. However, this is only true in terms of mundane technology. The discovery of mass-energy equivalence has also led to the development of atom bombs, which have the potential to cause mass destruction. Bioweapons, world poverty, and global warming are just a few of the other problems that have arisen alongside these unprecedented scientific breakthroughs.

How come a so-called advanced civilisation gave birth to such an evil-twin? The reason lies in the following example: A knife when used by an expert cuts vegetables whereas when used by a novice has the danger of cutting the finger. The same is the case with the modern world. The world is currently inexperienced in how to use the knife of wisdom - The West due its spiritual infancy and The East due to its slow cultural decay. But the East has in its womb of memories, many diamonds that could shine some light in these morally dark times.

The Patañjali Yoga-sutras is one such diamond of inexplicable merit, the nature of which will become clear to the reader as they progress through the following pages. However, the sūtras offer a solution to the world problem, in that it causes the Yogi to realize the One true Self shining through all as a common thread, leading to perceive the world as a single garland of beautiful flowers. Who would wish to pluck a flower from a beautiful garland? Thus, the causes of war and hatred would perish, and mutual trust and human bond would develop. This would give birth to the twin of ALL-GOOD, rather than the evil-twin, and the whole world would become a paradise.

A series of single drops form an ocean. Similarly, a change in the attitude of an individual alone transforms the world into a heaven on Earth! Therefore, let us understand the Yoga-sutras at a personal level. The book is for "YOU" - the practitioner of Yoga. Expect the changes in you and let Nature (or God) take care of changing the world. If we correct ourselves, the immediate company learns from us and the sequence of chain reactions continues to rectify the whole world - if not in a day, in a few years!

At an individual level, Yoga-sūtras provide a systematic approach to identify the root cause of all our problems, which is the alterations of behavior of the MIND. It then offers a solution to eliminate these changes (*chitta-vṛtti nirodhaḥ*). This solution is not a brute force method, but rather a way of developing a habit of staying blissful, which leads to clarity of the self within. However, Patañjali warns that in the process of Yoga-path, one may encounter so-called obstacles (Yoga siddhis or supernatural powers). These obstacles can tempt the good in us to venture into evil. Only those who refrain from heeding to these impulses can lead the life of true bliss.

In consideration of these thoughts, I have commented upon the sutras in such a manner that they are easily understood by most of us without the use of much technical jargon. An attempt is made to explain and simplify the complex Sanskrit words without destroying the original import. Ample examples, sets of practices, types of meditations, etc., are given where necessary to make the intent of Sage Patañjali sink into our planes of comprehension.

May this book serve as a guide for young people who are seeking to understand the nature of reality, college students who are struggling with everyday challenges (such as grades, relationships, and bad habits), parents who are trying to set a good example for their children, and older adults who are looking to accelerate their spiritual growth through the lens of their life experiences.

I humbly dedicate this work to my revered Guru - Master E. K, who has shown me the way to the TRUTH through his teachings, grace and conscious presence.

- Dr. Tejaswi Katravulapally, PHD.

# 1. अथ योगानुशासनम्

## atha yogānuśāsanam

atha = *the following* ; yogānuśāsanam = *instructions on Yoga.*

*The following pertains to the set of instructions on the path of Yoga.*

The term "Anuśāsanam" is commonly translated as an explanation or exposition. However, Patañjali's perspective on this term differs as he solely provides direct and concise instructions and recommendations. Therefore, a more accurate interpretation of "Anuśāsanam" is INSTRUCTIONS. These instructions specifically pertain to Yoga, the path of Yoga to be exact. Throughout the work, numerous instructions are offered that can be implemented in daily life to assist individuals in living a genuine life aligned with the principles of Yoga.

## 2. योगश्चित्तवृत्तिनिरोधः

## yogaścittavṛttinirodhaḥ

yogaḥ = *Yoga;* citta+vṛtti = *alterations of mind;* nirodhaḥ = *stopping*

*Yoga is the art of stopping the alterations of mind.*

## 3. तदा द्रष्टुः स्वरूपेऽवस्थानम्

## tadā draṣṭuḥ svarūpesvasthānam

tadā = *then;* draṣṭuḥ = *the observer;* sva+rūpe = *form of the self;* avasthānam = *dwell*

*Then the observer (in us) starts to dwell in the form of the self.*

## 4. वृत्तिसारूप्यमितरत्र

## vṛttisārūpyamitaratra

vṛitti + sārūpyam = *identification with the object;* itaratra = *otherwise.*

*Otherwise, we get identified with the objects of senses or the associated thoughts of the mind.*

The mind often identifies with what it perceives through its senses and its thoughts. For example, if we buy a new car and it gets a dent, we may feel agitated or upset. This is because our mind has identified with the car. Similarly, if we are rejected from a job we wanted, we may feel disappointed or even depressed. This is because our mind has identified with the idea of getting the job.

Yoga can help us to stop the mind from identifying with anything other than the true self. This is done through a series of techniques that help to calm the mind and bring it to a state of stillness. When the mind is still, it is no longer able to identify with anything else. Yoga is not a set of postures or a series of exercises. **Yoga is a way of life** that is designed to help us live in harmony with ourselves and with the world around us.

The mind responds to stimuli from the environment and its own thoughts. Yoga can help us stop the reactions of the mind, making it less contaminated. This allows the perceiver within us to dwell in the true nature of the self.

Advaita philosophy teaches us how to intellectually separate the observer from the observed. For example, when a tree is observed - the eye becomes the observer. If the eye is observed - the mind becomes the observer. If the mind is observed, - the discriminative will (Buddhi) becomes the observer. If Buddhi is observed - the self becomes the observer. This flow of logic clearly shows how the true self in us is the actual Draṣṭu - Observer. The yoga-sutra states that this observer is all that remains when the mind's distortions cease. This is what is meant by the observer "dwells in the form of true self" as a result of the "cessation of numerous activities of the mind."

Imagine a lake with many ripples. When the ripples stop, the mud settles and the shiny pebbles underneath become visible. Similarly, when the mind stops its "monkey-like" activity of jumping from one thought to another, the true self shines forth. By stopping the alterations to the mind, we are successful in recognising our true self. But if we do not stop the mental modifications, the mind assumes the form of the object it gets associated with - be it a sensual object or a mental thought-object. Then, the pains and pleasures of such association are felt as if real and the jīva (being) in us starts to suffer the consequences.

Consider this: While dreaming, imagine that someone has stolen our prized possession, say a gold ring. In the dream, we become agitated, and this agitation even manifests in the real world as a rapid breath and bodily movements in sleep. However, when we wake up, we realize that it was only a dream, and the agitation subsides. Similarly, when the mind is in its identified state with everything except the true self within, suffering is definitely experienced and this affects the reality of our existence. However, when the mind turns inward, as mentioned before, none of the objects or events can affect us, and our reality becomes an unshakable bliss.

## 5. वृत्तयः पञ्चतय्यः क्लिष्टाक्लिष्टाः

## vṛttayaḥ pañcatayyaḥ kliṣṭākliṣṭāḥ

vṛittayaḥ = *the vṛttis are;* pañcatayyaḥ = *of five types;*

kliṣṭāḥ + akliṣṭāḥ = *they are also complex or simple.*

**The vṛttis of mind are five types. Each of them is either complex or simple.**

## 6. प्रमाणविपर्ययविकल्पनिद्रास्मृतयः

## pramāṇa-viparyaya-vikalpa-nidrā-smṛtayaḥ

**The five vṛittis of the mind are : Pramāṇa, Viparyaya, Vikalpa, Nidrā and Smṛti.**

The five types of behaviors of the mind will be discussed in the following sūtras. However, Patañjali informs us that each of them can be either complex or simple. The complexity or simplicity of a behavior is determined by our involvement with the situation, not by the absolute nature of things.

For example, suppose we are sitting for meditation. At that moment the phone rings, or a child rings the doorbell, or a delivery person knocks at the door. In each of these scenarios, we have a choice (in terms of our attitude) to respond calmly and do what is necessary, or to angrily complain and curse the interruptions. One is the simple side of the mind, and the other is the complex side of the same coin.

Therefore, in any of the vṛittis that will be described later, the mind can either react positively (akliṣṭa) or negatively (kliṣṭa). The goal is to train our attitude to be oriented in the positive (akliṣṭa) way.

The names of the five types of vṛttis are

- Pramāṇa
- Viparyaya
- Vikalpa
- Nidra
- Smṛti

Each of these five terms should be understood in a scientific sense. We should not use dictionary definitions, but rather the definitions given by Patañjali himself in the following sūtras.

# *Alteration-1: Right Measure*

## 7. प्रत्यक्षानुमानागमाः प्रमाणानि

## pratyakṣānumānāgamāḥ pramāṇāni

pratyakṣa = *direct measure;* anumāna = *inference;* āgama
= *the true nature;* pramāṇāni = *is pramāṇa.*

*Pramāṇa is to "know" something by: direct measure
(via senses), indirect measure (inference) or by the
measure of the-word.*

The actual meaning of pramāṇa "right measure". Here,
measure doesn't pertain to the physical dimension alone, but
the totality of the object under consideration "as - it - is".
So "to know as it is" is synonymous to "right measure" in its
scientific sense of the word Pramāṇa.

We perceive objects through our senses, and then we
understand them by processing the information that our
senses send to our brain. For example, when we see a tree in
front of our house, the information that our eyes send to
our brain allows us to know if the tree is green or
brown. This is called **Direct-Measure (pratyakṣa-pramāṇa)**.
[**Prati** = in front of and **Akṣa** = eyes => senses].

To understand the aspects of objects that are not directly perceptible, we use the faculty of the brain that can infer a particular aspect of an object based on an indirect inference made upon another aspect of the same object. For instance, if we see smoke rising high into the sky, we can infer that there must have been fire at its ground-point. Therefore, by seeing the smoke, we can conclude that there is fire. Such measure of knowledge is **_Indirect-Measure (anumāna-pramāṇa)._**

There is another way to gain knowledge about something. It is through the statement of a credible source. For example, we read in a newspaper that there was an earthquake in a certain location. We believe this because we trust the newspaper. This type of knowledge acquisition is called **Word-Measure (Āgama-pramāṇa).**

All pramāṇas also have a deeper significance. At first, we perceive the world through direct measurement, which is our natural inclination. We do not believe in anything that is beyond the scope of our senses. Therefore, GOD or anything spiritual is just a fable to us. As we progress through our evolutionary cycles, we gain intuition and begin to sense the presence of hidden deities or powers that govern the laws of nature. As we continue to evolve, we enter a realm where we can perceive the utterance of creation in its purest form. In other words, we can comprehend the laws of nature in their original language, before they are translated into our regular language. This is the true Āgama or Veda or The WORD, according to the scriptures.

In a sense, the Pramāṇa vṛtti in its rudimentary stage obscures the truth and makes our lives complicated (kliṣṭa way). However, the same vṛtti can also help us progress spiritually and gain access to the word of God in its progressive stages (akliṣṭa way). This is what Patañjali alluded to when he spoke of the complexity and simplicity of the vṛttis.

# Alteration-2: Wrong Measure

## 8. विपर्ययो मिथ्याज्ञानमतद्रूप प्रतिष्ठं

### *viparyayo mithyājñānamatadrūpa pratiṣṭham*

viparyayaḥ = *wrong measure;* mithya = *false;* jñānam = *knowledge;* atadrūpa = *not its form;* pratiṣṭham = *established.*

*Viparyaya (wrong measure) is establishing in the false knowledge of that which is not its own form*

When one doesn't use the aforementioned Pramāṇas carefully, one falls prey for the wrong measure or Viparyaya. Basically it acts as a NOT-gate to whatever information our senses perceive

Say, **A** is our friend. We can see that **A** is a human being. We can make an educated guess about how **A** will behave in a given situation. We can trust **A's** word based on the word of a mutual friend.

However, our mind's mental state of Viparyaya superimposes a false layer of perception on **A**. We begin to see **A** not as a mere human being, but as "our close associate" and as "our close friend". But is **A** absolutely "ours"? No! It is only a relative truth. The equation of being "our" is a truth value that is valid only for us, and not for everyone.

This relative, secluded, and constrained false perception of our surroundings is called **Wrong-Measure (Viparyaya)**.

This falsity of the world around us is called *Mithya* and the knowledge pertaining to it is called *Mithyā-Jñānam*. If we look closely, most of us are always in this false-knowledge only. As long as this Viparyaya exists, one lives under the false-impression of delusory reality (kliṣṭa way).

If viparyaya is utilized properly, it can be beneficial. For instance, the student-guru relationship is false in an absolute sense due to the truth of oneness of all, but it is necessary for the disciple to progress by training under a guru. Similarly, the relationships we have with others can be used to uplift them on the path of self-realization by cultivating a group habit of self-inquiry or meditation, etc. This is the positive side of Viparyaya (akliṣṭa way).

## 9. शब्दज्ञानानुपाती वस्तुशून्यो विकल्पः

## śabdajñānānupātī vastuśūnyo vikalpaḥ

śabda = *word;* jñāna + anupāti = *following the inference;*
vastu = *object;* śūnyo = *being non-existent;* vikalpaḥ =*is*
*empty measure.*

*Vikalpa (empty measure) is the knowledge that follows the inference based on the word whose object is non-existent.*

Consider the phrase "Green Sky." What does this combination of words conjure up in our mind? Both words are meaningful, but when put together, they create an unrealistic image. Let's take this a step further and say "the 9th fundamental color" or "the 9th fundamental musical note." Previously, we could at least imagine a green sky. But now, it is impossible to even conceive of what is being spoken of, even though every word and sentence is grammatically correct. Knowledge that is gained from words that have no real-world counterpart to the object being referred to is known as **Empty-Measure (vikalpa)**.

In our ordinary lives, we discuss the future, which has not yet come, and we discuss possibilities. Even though these things are not real, our minds respond to them. Sometimes, even when an object is real, its absence in front of us can be brought to life by simply saying its name. This is also Vikalpa. For example, we are studying for an exam and the name of an actor appears in our book, which can trigger a flurry of thoughts about the movie he acted in. This reaction of the mind to the virtual presence of an object, triggered by a word, is **Vikalpa**. Patañjali warns us about this. (kliṣṭa way).

On the path of Yoga, Vikalpa is an interesting tool that helps us to gain a basic understanding of the concept of God. Before we can fully realize God or Atman, the idea is essentially "Vastu-Śūnya" for us. However, we must start somewhere, and so if we use Vikalpa to focus our minds on our own personal definition of God, we can gradually progress along the path of yoga and experience chitta-vṛtti nirodha. This is when our thoughts about God cease to exist, and we instead become one with God. Our earlier thoughts about God are then completely erased by the light of this newfound truth (akliṣṭa way).

## 10. अभावप्रत्ययालम्बना वृत्तिर्निद्रा

## abhāva pratyayālambanā vṛttirnidrā

abhāva = *absence of mind-stuff;* pratyaya = *related to;*

ālambana = *anchor;* vṛtti = *alteration of mind;* nidrā = *sleep.*

*Nidrā is that alteration of mind which pertains to anchoring (of mind) in the absence of mind-stuff.*

Sleep is a state of mind where there are no reactions to the surroundings because the input signals from the surroundings are cut off. There is no sense of "I am" in sleep. Does this mean that sleep is the same as Chitta-Vṛtti nirodha, the goal of Yoga? There is a key difference between the two states that should be noted.

Patanjali defines Nidra as a Vṛtti. One may wonder how can the absence of thoughts or reactions of the mind be a Vṛtti. When we are asleep, we are not aware that we are asleep. However, when we wake up, we know that we were asleep. The faculty or the Vṛtti of the mind that allows us to know that we were asleep is called NIDRĀ. This Vṛtti is anchored to the state of absence of mind-stuff. In other words, this Vṛtti compares the waking state to the state that had no mind-stuff (thoughts, ideas, etc.) and reminds us of the experience. This means that, in normal sleep, the mind is not completely asleep, because there is a Vṛtti that is continuously registering the experience of temporary absence of thoughts and conveying it to us when we wake up. It is the same Vṛtti that puts us to sleep every day and pushes us into unconscious states when we are in extreme danger (kliṣṭa way).

"Are the states of Nidrā and Citta-Vṛtti Nirodha similar?". We can confidently assert that they are not. When the ultimate goal of Yoga is achieved, we stop nidrā along with other vṛttis. Does that mean we no longer sleep? The answer is no. We still sleep, but not in the absence of mind-stuff (nidrā). Instead, we enter a state of Yoga-Nidrā, which is a state of poise and calmness obtained through dissolving into the true Self - *ALL-present* (akliṣṭa way).

## 11. अनुभूतविषयासंप्रमोषः स्मृतिः

## anubhūtaviṣayāsampramoṣaḥ smṛtiḥ

**anubhūta = *experienced;* viṣayā = *objects of senses;* a +**

**sam + pramoṣa = *not being distorted;* smṛtiḥ = *is***

**remembrance.**

*Remembrance is the retention of past experiences of objects of mind without being distorted (as-it-were).*

Consider this: today, we were invited to a Rajasthani wedding and we had a wonderful time eating their dal-bati-churma. We returned home, and suddenly, we had a strong desire to eat the dish again. In fact, we began to savor the flavor in our mouths, even though the dal-bati-churma was no longer in front of us. This alteration to our minds, which allows us to repeatedly experience the objects of our senses even when they are not present, is known as Smṛti.

Our thoughts often dwell on the past or future. When they dwell on the past, it is due to smṛti, and when they dwell on the future, it is due to vikalpa. We often dwell on the past more than the future because the past has already happened and we are sure of it. This means that smṛti is a more powerful vṛtti. The sadness of losing someone, the fear or phobia of something, etc. are all caused by smṛti (kliṣṭa way).

However, like all other vṛttis, smṛti also has a positive side. We are able to love and help each other because of the memories we have of our interactions with others. Nidrā (sleep) is only possible because of smṛti's ability to recall the experience. We are able to follow the teachings of our Guru because of smṛti. In fact, at a certain stage of aṣṭānga Yoga, when we begin to experience certain degree of the mental-poise, it is smṛti that remains with us until the final cessation of all vṛttis. This allows us to remember the sweet experience of Self and inspires us to strive to make such an experience permanent (akliṣṭa way).

Though the vṛitti of memory is essential for our day-to-day life, it will be ceased by the path of yoga in the end. This does not imply that we will forget our names and other details, or become patients with memory loss. In the yogic state of ultimate realization of the true self as one, smṛti will cease to function because there is no second object to be recollected in that state. All of our details, associations, and so on still exist, but they are now subsumed under the umbrella of oneness. Our memory will be so sharp that we will even be able to recall details from our past lives or the lives of others. However, we will not perceive these details as separate entities from us, but rather as part of ourselves. This is the distinction between an individual's memory and a true Yogi's memory.

## 12. अभ्यासवैराग्याभ्यां तन्निरोधः

### abhyāsavairāgyābhyāṃ tannirodhaḥ

abhyāsa = *by abhyāsa;* vairāgyābhyām = *and by vairāgya;*

tat = *that;* norodhaḥ = *is stopped.*

*By abhyāsa and vairāgya that (alteration of mind) is stopped.*

We have observed that the objective of yoga is to prevent the mind from becoming agitated. According to Patanjali, this can be accomplished with the assistance of two essential methods: **Abhyāsa** and **Vairāgya**

# Method-1: Relentless Effort

## 13. तत्र स्थितौ यत्नोऽभ्यासः

## tatra sthitau yatnosbhyāsaḥ

tatra = *in the state;* sthitau = *state;* yatnaḥ = *continued effort;* abhyāsaḥ = *is abhyāsa.*

*To remain in that state of cittavṛtti nirodha by a continued effort (of WILL) is Abhyāsa.*

## 14. स तु दीर्घकालनैरन्तर्यसत्कारासेवितो दृढभूमिः

## sa tu dīrghakāla nairantarya

## satkārāsevito dṛḍhabhūmiḥ

sa: tu = *that indeed;* dīrgha+kāla = *for a long time;* nairantarya = *without any breaks;* satkāra = *noble deeds;* āsevitaḥ = *practiced;* dṛḍha+bhūmiḥ = *firm grounding.*

*That (abhyāsa) will take a firm ground (stability) when noble deeds are practiced without any breaks for a long time.*

Abhyāsa means repeated practice over a long period of time without breaks. This is one of the keys to mastering any skill. Our own lives began with Abhyāsa. We learned to walk, talk, draw, calculate, and so on through Abhyāsa.

The goal of Yoga is to stop the fluctuations of the mind. This can be achieved by constantly suggesting this idea to ourselves through the mind. Just as the ground must be stable and firm to plant a seed, so too the mind must be stable to sow the seeds of Abhyāsa.

The mind is a fluctuating entity, so how can we make it stable? The answer is to perform good deeds continuously and willfully. What constitutes a "good deed" is understood from the dharma śāstrās (scriptures on dharma) and is also indicated later by Patañjali as yama and niyama. In essence, the only way to achieve a disciplined mind and a deep-rooted sense of poise is through a moral life that is characterized by service to others.

So **Abhyāsa** is
1. The art of implementing an incessant, uninterrupted, continued and wilful effort.
2. Practicing the art of performing good deeds, in the aforementioned way, would strengthen the soul-idea of Abhyāsa.

**15.** दृष्टानुश्रविकविषयवितृष्णस्य वशीकारसंज्ञा वैराग्यम्

## dṛṣṭānuśravikaviṣayavitṛṣṇasya

## vaśīkārasañjñā vairāgyam

dṛṣṭa = *seen;* anuśravika = *heard;* viṣaya = *things;*

vitṛṣṇasya = *to the one who is free from yearning;* vaśīkāra

= *become a master (able to control);* sañjñā = *sign;*

vairāgyam = *detachment.*

*When a person is free from yearning the things of seen and heard (sensual things) it is the sign of mastery over detachment.*

## **16.** तत्परं पुरुषख्यातेर्गुणवैतृष्ण्यम्

## tatparaṃ puruṣakhyāterguṇavaitṛṣṇyam

tat + param = *that beyond;* puruṣa + khyāteḥ = *permeation of con-sciousness;* guṇa + vaitṛṣṇyam = *no yearning of qualities.*

*The highest form of that (vairāgyam) is to have no yearning for the qualitative world because of having tasted the permeating consciousness.*

In order to perform a good deed as a service, the mind must develop the habit of non-attachment to "What we have" and instead try to understand "What we are."

According to scriptures (like Taittirīya Upaniṣad, etc.), the human constitution is composed of five sheaths.

1. **Annamaya Kośa:** The Physical Layer
2. **Prāṇamaya Kośa:** The Vital Layer
3. **Manomaya Kośa:** The Mental Layer
4. **Vijñānamaya Kośa:** The Buddhic Layer
5. **Ānandamaya Kośa:** The All-Permeating Pure Bliss.

Layers 1, 2, and 3 are the lower domain, while Layer 4 is the higher domain. Layer 5 is the all-permeating layer that is truly ourselves.

In this framework of understanding, our attachment first begins with physical objects (annamaya), then the allure we find in their functionality (prāṇamaya), and finally the mind's fascination with the excessive use of these alluring functions (manomaya). For instance, let's say we buy a new laptop. At first, we are attached to the laptop itself as a possession. Over time, we become addicted to its functionality. Eventually, our thoughts begin to wander to upgrading it, redesigning it, or buying a new one. If this laptop were suddenly taken from us, we would likely become angry or upset. This is the nature of attachment.

When the mind is trained through practice (abhyāsa) to focus on mental equilibrium through good deeds, the usefulness of an object (such as the laptop in the previous example) exists for us only in its utilitarian value in the present moment, not in its alluring qualities. This leads to non-attachment in all three lower layers of existence, meaning that we are free from the lower domain of attachment.

As this practice strengthens, the mental waves gradually decrease, and the fourth layer, Buddhi (discriminative will), begins to influence the mind. Since Buddhi is the direct conduit to the fifth layer, BLISS, the mind begins to experience bliss, however small the dose may be. This is tasting the highest consciousness (*tat param puruṣakhyāte*), and one no longer even considers the lower associations (*guṇa vaitṛṣṇyam*).

So **Vairāgya** is

> a. *Lower*: The art of detaching oneself from the sensual objects, not yearning for their qualitative aspects and gaining a mastery over the same.

b. *Higher*: The art of acquiring the detachment by tasting the higher consciousness within, where the **wilful effort becomes an effortless Will**.

## 17. वितर्कविचारानन्दास्मितानुगमात् सम्प्रज्ञातः

## vitarka-vicāra-ānanda-asmita-anugamāt-samprajñātaḥ

vitarka = *reasoning (exterior);* vicāra = *contemplating (interior);* ānanda = *(deeper) happiness;* asmita = *realization of self within;* anugmāt = *by following;* samprajñātaḥ = *(detachment) with awareness.*

*The highest form (of non-attachment) is achieved by traveling from the exterior reasoning to interior contemplating to deeper happiness to realization of self within. Having all-awareness in this journey is called Samprajñāta - Vairāgyam.*

The highest level of non-attachment (vairāgya) is achieved when one begins to experience the highest consciousness. According to Patañjali, this occurs in two stages. The first stage is being described here. This process can be summarized as follows:

1. Observe the objects, people, and our relationship
   with them. Then, reason through (**Vitarka**):
      - All objects are made up of atoms, which are in
        turn modes of energy.
      - Energy is the power of consciousness.
      - Continue reasoning until we reach the
        conclusion that all-permeating consciousness
        is the ultimate substratum.

2. Hold the logical thought that the intellect has
   reached and push it through the limits of intuition via
   contemplation (**Vicāra**):
      - This contemplation should happen all the time.
      - Every act we perform and every associated
        thought that is germinated must have this
        contemplation as its backdrop.

3. After a certain stage, one reaches a state of
   contentment with the held-up logic. A firm belief and
   understanding is developed about the idea of the
   highest consciousness. This brings in peace and
   happiness (**Ānanda**).

4. This happiness leads to realization of the self within
   (**Asmita**) - not as an idea but as an experience.

All of these four stages occur with a sense that "I am experiencing," "I am feeling this higher consciousness," "Now I have the clarity of being," etc. The individual sense of "I am" exists, and this is the first kind of dispassion called **Samprajñāta-Vairāgyam**. Sam+Prajñāta = Having the sense of "I am" intact.

## 18. विरामप्रत्ययाभ्यासपूर्वः संस्कार शेषोऽन्यः
## virāmapratyayābhyāsapūrvaḥ saṃskāra śeṣosnyaḥ

virāma = *comes to stop;* pratyaya = *perception;*

abhyāsa+pūrvaḥ = *having incessantly practiced before;*

saṃskāra+śeṣaḥ = *leaving the associations;* anyaḥ = *the*

*other (stage).*

***Having preceded by relentless - continuous - effort, the other stage (of vairāgya) is achieved when the perceptions come to stop and any remaining associations are left off.***

The first stage of Vairāgya begins with an outward journey that eventually leads inward. Throughout this process, the observer and their opinions remain intact. This should continue for an extended period of time without any interruptions. This process is known as Abhyāsa. After a great deal of Abhyāsa in the first stage of Vairāgya, one enters the second stage, which is characterized by two primary elements:

1. **The shedding of associations.** As we travel inward, many ideas and opinions become woven into our

contemplative mind. These are known as saṃskāras. These saṃskāras must be shed, but they should not be shed through conscious effort. Rather, they should be shed naturally, like a fruit falling from a tree when it is ripe.

2. **The cessation of all perceptions.** This means that the mind will experience a state of stillness, like a ripple-free surface.

A helpful analogy for understanding these two stages (sūtras 18 and 19) is to imagine a fruit that we have never tasted before. We might first consult a dictionary to learn about its description. Then, we might ask a few people about its taste. We would continue in this way until we had exhausted all of the information "about" the fruit. This is similar to the samprajñāta stage of Vairāgya. However, when we finally take a bite of the fruit and are completely lost in its flavor, we will experience the taste as being inseparable from ourselves. We will have no words to describe it afterward. Even while tasting the fruit, we should strive to reach a state where the triangle of taster-taste-tasted collapses into unity.

This second stage of Vairāgya is known as **Asamprajñāta Vairāgya**, which means *"the detachment that comes from the absence of the sense of individual being."* In this stage, there will only be actions from the being and existence, but no reactions or no sense of "I am -".

*Note: The two stages are often interpreted as stages of samādhi with seed (sabīja samādhi) in the commentaries to Yoga-sutrās. This interpretation is inaccurate. If an important concept like samādhi were being introduced, Patañjali would have coined the word. However, the word samādhi is not used at all in this context. Additionally, it is illogical for Patañjali to suddenly skip to samādhi and then return to other concepts after discussing the previous stage of vairāgya. Therefore, Samprajñāta and the later stage (asamprajñāta) pertain to vairāgya, not samādhi.*

## 19. भवप्रत्ययो विदेह प्रकृतिलयानाम्

## bhavapratyayo videha prakṛtilayānām

bhavapratyayaḥ = *to be bron again;* videha = *without bodies;* prakṛtilayānām = *merged with nature.*

***Those (who practice yoga) without bodies or those who merge with nature, will be born again.***

Bhava-Pratyaya means to be born again. Two kinds of practice-paths are described here which inevitably results in re-birth over and over again.

1. Videha
2. Prakṛtilaya

Videha is a state of being without a body. One may interpret this in many ways, such as through the concept of devas or celestial beings or departed souls, etc. However, if we consider that the Yoga Sutras of Patanjali are meant for our practice in this life and "at this moment," then all such interpretations are unnecessary, regardless of their validity.

In this light, we can understand videha as those who have left the body. What does this mean? As long as we see ourselves as separate from our bodies, we will eventually leave the body and be reborn. Only when we realize that there is no separation between ourselves and our bodies, i.e., when we achieve oneness, will there be no rebirth. Videhas are those who have not yet fully realized that the body is part of their unified existence. For instance, a senior yoga practitioner may enjoy eating roti with tomato dal, even though this is not a healthy diet. This shows that the practitioner still has some attachment to the body, as the taste of this food is imprinted on their mental planes and will be carried as samskāra into the next life. However, if the practitioner is truly advanced in their yoga practice, they will have no special favorites in their diet and will eat only what is necessary for the body.

**Prakṛtilayā** is the state of being merged with nature and its splendors. Let us take an example: For a regular yet staunch devotee of Viṣṇu, the idol of sleeping Viṣṇu in Śrirangam gives ecstasy and joy. The same idol was visited by Ādi Śankarācārya and the same ecstasy was felt by him. The difference lies in that, for the devotee, God exists only in the idol and anything other than the idol is different from the concept of Viṣṇu. But for Ādi Śankaracārya, God existed even in the idol (along with himself and the creation around him as a part of THAT). The devotee is said to be in Prakṛtilayā, while Śankarācārya is said to be in true Samādhi.

Videha is the path of perceiving indifference through internal difference, while Prakṛtilaya is the external path of merging with nature while still maintaining a sense of many. Both of these paths lead to rebirth because the self is still under the illusion that it is separate from other things.

Patañjali indirectly warns us that the vairāgya states mentioned in the previous sūtrās are not the final objective. They are only steps on the path of yoga. After achieving asamprajñāta vairāgya, there may be a temptation to believe that we have attained samādhi (on whose meaning we are yet to be instructed by Patañjali). However, Patañjali stops us here and asks us to examine if we have achieved videha and prakṛtilayā by any chance. In other words, are we still experiencing a separation between the inside and the outside worlds? If so, then we still have work to do on our path. Otherwise, the question does not even arise because we have already achieved unity,

## 20. श्रद्धावीर्यस्मृतिसमाधिप्रज्ञापूर्वक इतरेषाम्

## śraddhā-vīrya-smṛti-samādhi-

## prajñā pūrvaka itareṣām

śraddha = *dedication;* vīrya = *strong effort;* smṛti = *remembrance;* samādhi = *attainment;* prajña = *(awareness of) higher consciousness;* pūrvaka = *preceded by;* itareṣām = *the others.*

*The others enter samādhi (attainment) by a sincere dedication, strong wilful effort, constant remembrance and awareness of the higher consciousness.*

Those who are not of the nature of Bhava-Pratyaya (videha and prakṛtilayānām) will attain Samādhi. Patañjali has not yet disclosed what samādhi is. Samādhi, derived from the Sanskrit terms "Sam" (together), "ā" (towards), and "dhi" (to hold or place), literally means "to hold together in oneness." Thus, Samādhi = Attainment i.e., attainments of a state of unity with all aspects of existence.

This is the first time he has used the word, and therefore, we too need to understand only as much as he mentions.

**After achieving para-vairāgya, the following elements help us enter the state of Samādhi:**

1. **Śraddha:** Sincere dedication that shields us from distractions on the path.
2. **Vīrya:** Strong and potent effort that pushes our boundaries into the vast domains of higher yogic states.
3. **Smṛti:** Constant remembrance and recollection of the pursuit we have embarked upon.
4. **Prajña:** Awareness of higher consciousness as it manifests its presence through us (by burning the veil of Maya or illusion).

These elements will lead to the experience of Samādhi. Initially, this experience may be fleeting. However, by maintaining our dedication, effort, remembrance and awareness, we can perpetuate the state of Samādhi to eternity. This is what a Yogi who aims at no-rebirth (liberation) needs to do.

****Note:**_The state of Samādhi is contrasted with Bhava-pratyaya. This contrast implies that a sense of no re-birth can be understood as a consequence of Samādhi. In this context, no re-birth means that the body may be reborn, but the being within does not experience rebirth (there is continuity of conscious existence)._

*Consider the descent of Lord Krishna. Although his body was born at the time of his so-called birth, his presence had been present since the dawn of time. He is the very awareness that we call I AM in all. So, can we say that God took birth at all? No! Yet we say that Krishna took birth because we look at things from our lens of perception. For those of us who are in duality (non-samādhi), bhava-pratyaya is the result. We see many births and we experience many births. But for those who have attained the ultimate goal of Samādhi, there are no births. Yet, these beings descend into bodies from the universal ocean of existence, like ice-cubes solidify from water. They guide the younger beings in evolution. But all the while, they live in the state of God-realization. This is what we understand when we study with sincerity the lives of many saints.*

# Different Styles in Achieving Samādhi

## 21. तीव्रसंवेगानामासन्नः

### tīvrasamvegānāmāsannaḥ

tīvra = *intense;* samvegānām = *at a good speed;* āsannaḥ = *comes.*

*Samādhi is achieved more quickly when the aforementioned elements (in the previous sutra) are implemented with greater intensity.*

## 22. मृदुमध्याधिमात्रत्वात् ततोऽपि विशेषः

### mṛdu-madhya-adhimātratvāt tatospi viśeṣaḥ

mṛdu = *soft;* madhya = *medium;* adhimātratvāt = *Hard (too much);* tataḥ + api = *in that also;* viśeṣaḥ = *differentiation;*

*Even within this intense application, there are finer stages of distinctions: soft, medium, and hard.*

The instructions are clear in theory. However, when it comes to practice, our personal biases (which are shaped by our experiences in this and past lives) can affect the amount of effort we put in. This can manifest in three ways:

1.  **Adhimātra:** A beginner on the yoga path may be overly enthusiastic and eager to see results quickly.

This can lead them to try to force things, which can be counterproductive.

2.  **Madhya:** As they progress, students may learn that trying to go too fast can actually backfire. This can teach them to relax and reduce the intensity of their efforts, both mentally and physically. However, their subtle will is strengthened by the positive effects they see over time.

3.  **Mṛdu:** Eventually, students who are able to balance their expectations and their dedicated practice will find themselves in a state of dynamic equilibrium. Things will flow smoothly, they will be able to enter deeper stages of meditation with less effort, and their will will become even stronger.

This strengthening of the will leading to speedy and easy attainment is what Patañjali refers to as **tīvra saṁvegānām**. It is not a matter of mental stress, but rather a matter of the will setting the habits, routines, and every aspect of the yoga practice into proper order. This is most fully realized in the Mṛdu style of approach.

# Method of Submission to The Lord

## 23. ईश्वरप्रणिधानाद्वा

## īśvarapraṇidhānādvā

īśvara = *The Lord;* praṇidhānāt = *total surrenderance;* vā = *or.*

*Or, the same (samādhi) is attained by a total surrenderance to The Lord.*

An alternate method is being described by Patañjali that can help us in achieving the goal of Yoga. It is "Surrenderance to The-Lord". The moment such an instruction is given, two questions arise

- What is surrenderance?

- Who is the Lord spoken here?

Surrendering means to offer the sense of ownership, doership and results of an action unto someone else. This releases us from the burden of Karma and purifies every attempt of doing because the attempt of an action is now not "by" us but "through" us. Of course, a mere thought is not sufficient, but surrenderance should be inculcated and mastered by devotion and love.

We can love and be devoted if we know whom we are submitting to! Therefore, Patañjali immediately describes who this Lord is in the next sūtras, so that we do not make our own definitions and get trapped in our own thought-maze.

**24.** क्लेशकर्मविपाकाशयैरपरामृष्टः पुरुषविशेष ईश्वरः

**kleṣa-karma-vipāka-āśayaiḥ-**

**aparāmṛṣṭaḥ-puruṣaviśeṣaḥ-īśvaraḥ**

kleṣa = *complexities;* karma = *actions;* vipāka = *resultants;*

āśayaiḥ = *intentions;* aparāmṛṣṭaḥ = *untouched (by the*

*above);* puruṣaviśeṣaḥ = *the special being;* īśvaraḥ = *The*

Lord.

*The Lord is the special being - the true I AM in all - who is untouched by any complexities or actions or resultants or intentions.*

**25.** तत्र निरतिशयं सर्वज्ञबीजं

**tatra niratiśayaṃ sarvajñabījam**

tatra = *there (in īśvara);* niḥ+atiśayam = *nothing can*

surpass; sarvajña+bījam = *seed of omniscience.*

*There is the seed of omniscience in Īśvara which can not be surpassed by anyone.*

**26.** पूर्वेषामपि गुरुः कालेनानवच्छेदात्

# pūrveṣāmapi guruḥ kālena-anavcchedāt

pūrveṣām = *for those who came before;* api = *indeed;*

guruḥ = *the (great) teacher;* kālena = *by time;* anavacchedāt

= *indivisible.*

*Īśvara is indeed the great teacher for those who came before us (the ancients) because he is indivisible by time (or not affected by time).*

Īśvara is said to be the one who is untouched by the following

- **Kleśa**: If we have a knee ache, we may complain about it while sitting. But when we are discussing an important topic or when we are asleep, we forget the pain. The pain resurfaces when we think about it. This shows that there is a part of us that is untouched by the pain. Extending the same logic to most of our life complexities, there is an aspect of us that is untouched by all our complexities, and that is Īśvara.

- **Karma**: Actions are the result of thoughts, and thoughts are the result of impulses from baggage of impressions from the past and present lives. When we take ownership of our actions, we are doomed to enjoy the fruits of those actions, whether they are good or bad. Either outcome will result in further entanglements, causing more impressions for actions, and this is a never-ending cycle. However, there is an Īśvara within us who is not performing any actions (as actions are performed in the ONE, like waves occur in an ocean). He is beyond actions and therefore beyond the fruits of actions.

- **Vipāka**: We were once young, now adults, and we'll be old in future. We were once little, now strong, and will be weak. These kinds of things that result in consequent attributes are called Vipākas. In all of these changes, our body and mind have changed, but the sense of

"I am so and so" has not changed. To whom are we pointing and saying "I am"? That intent and sense has not changed. That changeless entity amidst the changes is Īśvara and therefore is not affected by them.

- **Āśaya**: The intentions that have come forth in us are called Āśaya. "I want to become a millionaire," "I want to be a scientist," "I need to change the world," etc., are all intentions that have germinated in us. They affect the sense of individuality to some extent, bringing in more pride or happy success, etc. But the consciousness is not affected by these intentions. Whether the person was a non-millionaire in the beginning of his pursuit or a millionaire after his pursuit, whom we call "Person - Puruṣa" has not changed. Only his attributed social glory has changed in his mind. That which is untouched by any intentions is Īśvara.

Puruṣa means the one who resides in the creation (pura). However, when the word śeṣa is added, a more advanced meaning is implied. Śeṣa means a remainder. Vi+Śēṣa means that which has no remainder (completeness). It appears that Īśvara is the resident of the creation who has no remainder and is complete as a totality of UNITY. In other words, Īśvara is the all-permeating and all-encompassing cosmic person. Therefore, there can never be any remainder left even after the whole creation is born or destroyed. He remains as the ONE, and in him all changes occur. And because he is the totality, he remains Viśeṣa. Viśeṣa also means unique, as in the unique background consciousness that we enter into every day when we sleep and from which we wake up as an individual entity. This unique Puruṣa is referred to as Īśvara by Patañjali here.

The Lord is Omniscient (sarvajña), meaning He knows all things. Knowledge is the perception of events that occur in time and space through the mind. Who can know everything? Only the one who is the basis of all minds and the cosmic fabric of time and space. Therefore, Īśvara is the substratum and the very thread by which the space-time-mind fabrics are woven, and hence He is All-Knowing.

If the Lord is all-knowing, then his creation, being a part of him, must also have the seeds of omniscience. Just as a banyan tree seed contains all the information necessary to grow into a tree, which then produces more seeds, and so on, even though the Lord is all-knowing, his creation also contains the seeds of omniscience. This means that we, as part of creation, also have the seeds of omniscience within us. However, it is cautioned that we cannot surpass the Lord's omniscience. As one advances in the path of Yoga, they must not develop pride in their supranatural knowledge. Instead, they must remain humble and submit to Īśvara, remembering that a part cannot surpass the whole.

In a practical sense, this means that we have the innate ability to comprehend certain things. For instance, when we learn a math problem or a complicated legal situation, we can analyze and synthesize the explanation because we already possess the required knowledge. This is not something that is taught to us; rather, it is something that we are born with. When a baby learns math for the first time, it understands the concept of 1+1=2 even though it has never been taught this before. This is because the baby already has the knowledge of this concept, but it is dormant until it is awakened by a teacher.

This is why the word for teacher in our culture is "Guru." Guru means "the dispeller of darkness within." A Guru does not impart anything new; he simply dispels the darkness and we begin to realize things on our own. However, this is only possible because we all have the seeds of omniscience within us which are aiding in understanding things.

It is for this reason that it is said that Īśvara is the one and only greatest guru for all those who has born before since the dawn of time. While a physical guru may begin the process of removing the veil of illusion, it is Īśvara who grants us the ability to understand, know the light within, and experience the grand truth of who we are. As already stated, Īśvara is the creator of time, he stands beyond time and hence he is indivisible by time. Therefore according to Patañjali, Īśvara is the only guru for all and he is undisturbed by the eternal unwinding serpent of time.

# Om: The Divine Codec

## 27. तस्य वाचकः प्रणवः

## tasya vācakaḥ praṇavaḥ

tasya = *his;* vācakaḥ = *utterance;* praṇavaḥ = *Om.*

***The utterance of Īśvara is Om.***

The previous sūtras have stated that a profound and significant method to attain the goal of Yoga is to submit everything that "I have" to the Īśvara, the true "I AM." However, this is only the beginning step. After we have submitted, what do we do next? We would like to converse with that Lord and seek guidance, as he is also the true Guru to all those who have walked the path before. But how can we converse with the Īśvara, who is the all-pervading, all-knowing entity?

In this sūtra, the passcode to enter into the Kingdom of God is given. The sūtra has a two-fold meaning and hence two-fold application

1.  Lord utters the creation (us) as Om
2.  We utter the Lord as Om

When Īśvara creates the Universe, he does so using the potency of the sacred syllable Om. More on this has been expounded in Māṇḍūkya Upaniṣad[1] of Atharvaṇa Veda.

Since the creation originated from Om and is thus suffused with it, every atom of the creation vibrates at the same frequency as Om. This is the story of how creation came into being from the Lord. Because we are part of his creation, he has left us with this secret as the key to reach him. We must keep this fact in mind and chant Om aloud in order to begin to experience Om within ourselves. This will create a link between the individual and Īśvara, which will allow us to be immersed in the direct shower of grace and guidance.

Thus, Om is the means by which the Lord brought us into creation, and it is also the means by which we can merge back into him.

---

[1] The author has also published a short commentary on this work: Māṇḍūkya Upaniṣad - A Meditative Approach, available through Amazon and Notion Press.

## 28. तज्जपस्तदर्थभावनम्

### tat-japaḥ-tatartha-bhāvanam

tat = *that;* japaḥ = *repetitive utterance;* tat+artha = *meaning of that (om);*  bhāvanam = *contemplate.*

**Repeat that sacred syllable Om and contemplate on its meaning.**

## 29. ततः प्रत्यक्चेतनाधिगमोऽप्यन्तरायाभवश्च

### tataḥ-pratyakcetana-adhigamosapi-antarāya-abhāvaśca

tataḥ = *by (practicing) that;* pratyak= *which exists in all;* cetana = *consciousness;*  adhigama = *attained;* api = *as well as* ; antarāya = *obstacles;* a+bhāvaśca = *removed from existence.*

**By practicing the utterance of Om, one will attain the (realization of) consciousness that exists in all as well as any obstacles in the path would be removed from existence.**

Three references are inevitable in the context of practical instructions on meditation of Om:

1. Bhagavad Gita says "*Om ityekākṣaram brahma vyāharan....*" - Om is one syllable Mantra that denotes Brahman (The Lord).
2. Chandogya Upaniṣad says "*Om ityetadakṣaram Udgītam upāsīt....*" - Udgīta means to utter aloud.
3. Īśa Upaniṣad says, "*So`ham Asmi*"

These three give us the quintessential points to note to perform the practice of utterance of Om. First, we have to utter Om aloud without any hesitation. It is not a silent meditation that is prescribed. This is the Udgīta vidya.

Second, utter Om as a single syllable and not as A-U-M separately, which is usually suggested in few other paths. Upāsīt means to sit very near. While uttering this Om, one must hear it with their ears and hence try to be one with the utterance. This is the true meaning of sitting close to a Mantra.

Third, the key to merging with the Lord is in our breath. So`ham has two meanings.

1. Soham = So + Ham = S + O + Ha + M. Consonants are the physical bodies whereas the vowels are the life in the bodies according to Mantra Śastra. Dropping of the consonants, we are left with O + M = Om. Now linking this with the sound of breath i.e., So is the sound of inhalation and Ha is the sound of exhalation and M is the bindu indicating nāda or subtle sound as

undercurrent. Thus, Soham Asmi means, Om is the very existence which is breathing our life through us. By meditating on this aspect of Om while breathing and uttering Om aloud, we shall reach the Kingdom of God in no time!

2. So`ham = Saḥ + Aham. Saḥ means He. All that we point to other than ourselves is Saḥ. The Omnipresent lord who is present in all the exterior surroundings is Saḥ. Aham is the individual self who is interior to our understanding. In saying So`ham Asmi, the seer suggests that "I am He". Linking this as well with the meditation of Om, the process as well as the goal of Yoga will become solid and the approach becomes error free.

*In summary, Om needs to be uttered aloud, heard while uttering, in the background a contemplation should run on the question that how the breath is carrying out by itself (who am I) and the answer that we being Īśvara, the breath is being carried out by his grace and that in this rhythm of life exists the soul of life as OM!*

Another way to understand the sutra "Tat Japaḥ Tat Artha Bhāvanam" is to focus on the word "Bhāvanam." Bhāva can mean to think (in a lower sense) or contemplate (in a higher sense), but it can also mean to manifest. By contemplating on the word OM and the sound of its utterance, the meaning of Om (whose content is Īśvara - all-permeability) begins to manifest in our perception of the surroundings by virtue of its power. This is called **pratyak-cetana**.

This pratyak-cetana slowly leads to a state of indifference towards seemingly opposite things in life. In such a state, what is an obstacle to a yogi? Nothing exists as an obstacle. An obstacle is only a mental idea, but not a physical entity. This state of removed obstacles is called **antarāya-abhāva**.

For instance, consider a new year resolution to meditate at 6 a.m. and 6 p.m. every day. However, as soon as we begin, we are interrupted by office emails, a power outage causes us to sweat profusely, we get stuck in traffic on our way home, or we stay up late and do not wake up early. We become irritated and abandon our objective entirely, blaming the obstacles. However, for those who have practiced the art of Om meditation, the previously apparent obstacles will now expose their lack of discipline. Most of the obstacles are due to the mind's resistance to following a certain routine. And they would not be concerned about those that are beyond their control because they perceive the divine hand in everything. As a result, their minds are not agitated, and they may adjust their meditation schedule for the day without feeling guilty. This is the significance of removing obstacles: the genuine obstacles are our own mental entanglements, and they will begin to dissolve from our minds, rendering them nonexistent.

**30.** व्याधिस्तान्यसंशयप्रमादालस्य
अविरतिभ्रान्तिदर्शनालब्धभूमिकत्व
अनवस्थितत्वानिचित्तविक्षेपस्तेऽन्तरायाः

**vyādhi-stānya-saṃśaya-pramāda-ālasya-
avirati-bhrāntidarśana-alabdahūmikatva-
anavasthitatvāni-cittavikṣepāḥ-te-antarāyāḥ**

**vyādhi** = *disease;* **stānya** = *rigidity;* **saṃśaya** = *doubt;*
**pramāda** = *misunderstanding;* **ālasya** = *laziness;* **avirati** =
*having no gap;* **bhrānti+darśana** = *illusive perception;*
**alabdha+būmikatva** = *inability to achieve solid ground ;*
**anavasthi+tatvāni** = *nature of instability;* **citta+vikṣepāḥ** =
*wavering of the mind; te* = *these ;* **antarāyāḥ** = *are the*
*obstacles.*

*The following are the obstacles that cause the mind to
waver: disease (physical and non-physical),
negligence (of putting effort), doubting (the efficacy
of their effort), misunderstanding (one for the other),
having no gap (continuing old habits), perception via
illusion (of one as many), inability to achieve solid
ground (causes discouragement later on), nature of
instability (in WILL).*

# 31. दुःख दौर्मनस्याङ्गमेजयत्व श्वासप्रश्वासा विक्षेपसहभुवः

## duḥkha-daurmanasya-aṅgamejayatva-śvāsa-prasvāsā-vikṣepa-sahabhuvaḥ

duḥkha = *sorrow*; daurmanasya = *mental depression*; aṅgamejayatva = *instability of bodily parts*; *śvāsa+prasvāsa* = *inhalation & exhalation*; vikṣepa = *are (the aforementioned) waverings*; sahabhuvaḥ = *that are born at the same time*;

*The following are also born along with the aforementioned obstacles which cause the wavering of mind: sorrow (to situations outside), mental depression (internal melancholy), instability in the organs of the physical body (making physical poise impossible) and respiration (breathing issues, practice of breathing exercises difficult).*

On the path of progress in Yoga, Patañjali notes many impediments. It is crucial to be aware of these, as they may appear disguised and impede our progress. Such is the foresight of Patañjali's instructional style. It is the responsibility of an instructor to not only provide direction on how to travel a path, but also to warn of the pitfalls and traps along the way.

The obstacles have been categorized into two groups:

**Obstacles due to one's own misdoings**

1. **vyādhi (disease):** Most of the diseases occur due to self misbehaving with our own body and environment around. In the name of development we destroy the nature around us and in the name of glamor and prestige we destroy bodily health. This causes diseases. They lead to physical and mental discomfort which inturn leads to disturbance in the path of Yoga. *To avoid this, we have to follow basic health and healing guidelines as indicated by the scripture of Āyurveda - The Veda of LIFE.*

2. **stānya (rigidity):** For instance, if our guru instructs us to meditate for fifteen minutes every day at 6 a.m. and 6 p.m., we may come up with a million reasons to avoid it. We may question whether it is mandatory to meditate at those specific times. We may also ask why we cannot meditate at our leisure or if a minute of deep concentration would suffice instead of fifteen minutes. These thoughts arise because our minds are rigid and do not like to conform to a regular routine. We may also be rigid in our beliefs. This is known as stānya. *To make progress on our spiritual journey, we must overcome our stānya. We*

*must learn to discipline ourselves and be consistent with our practice. We must also be mindful of our thoughts and actions, and avoid giving in to rigidity.*

3. **saṃśaya (doubt)**: One of the most formidable obstacles in any journey is doubt. It is not the same as questioning, which can be a useful tool for determining the best course of action. Doubt, on the other hand, implies a disbelief or a sense of disagreement with the task at hand. Doubting before choosing a path can lead to helpful questioning, which can help us make the right decision. However, doubting while on the path indicates that our mind is indecisive and unable to stick to our original reasoning, which led us to choose the path in the first place. *Therefore, it is important to avoid doubting once we have chosen a path and to instead follow it with full sincerity and devotion in order to make progress.*

4. **pramāda (misunderstanding)**: When a guru says something, we may interpret it differently and believe that our interpretation is correct. This is called pramāda. It can happen when we are not paying attention or concentrating on what is being taught. Our thoughts may wander, and by the time we refocus, we may have missed important instructions

or cautions. We may only be left with a few of the instructions. *To avoid pramāda, we need to calm our thoughts and slowly resonate them with the guru's instructions. We should not be afraid to go back to the guru and check if we have understood everything correctly. Taking these steps will help us avoid pramāda.*

5. **ālasya (laziness):** When the will sets a high goal, the mind cannot keep up. The mind sets a small goal, but the body cannot keep up. When the will, mind, and body are out of sync, it is called laziness or Ālasya. For example, we may resolve to start reading the book "Autobiography of a Yogi." However, our mind keeps pulling us toward watching a Netflix film or taking a nap. While we are on the couch watching a Netflix film, we need to cook to eat. However, our body does not want to leave the comfort of the couch. This is the nature of Ālasya. *Ālasya is an obstacle on the path of Yoga and must be avoided by developing a strong habit of doing and prioritizing necessary things over desired things.*

6. **avirati (having no gap):** Virati: Pause or Cessation Avirati is the opposite of Virati. It means having no pause. When we are excited about learning something new, we often try to implement it and practice it

without any gap. This can lead to fatigue and over-exertion, which can eventually cause us to stop what we have started. Avirati can also permeate our minds, preventing us from taking the time to understand ourselves or our relationships. We may feel like we are always busy, even when we are not actually doing anything. When someone asks for our help or advice, we may automatically reply that we are busy. This is Avirati speaking! The only way to avoid Avirati is to start incorporating regular breaks into our lives. This includes taking breaks from work, as well as from our yoga practices. These breaks will help us to refresh and rejuvenate our minds and bodies. Virati is similar to Śavāsana, which is a yoga pose that is often used to relax the body and promote proper blood circulation and breath flow. Śavāsana is a time for us to rest and reflect on our practice.

7. **bhrāntidarśana (illusive perception):** When someone holds a rope in the dark, and it moves suddenly due to wind, they may perceive it as a snake. This can even cause heart attacks. Although it is a rope, the mind falsely believes it to be a snake (we call this in Sanskrit as "*rajju-sarpa-bhrānti*"). Similarly, as we progress on the path of yoga and attain supernatural powers, we may experience illusions and take these

illusions for absolute experiences of Yoga! For example, someone may dream of a god speaking to them in regards to how to cook potatoes. They may listen to everything the God says in the dream and feel it as real. They will start eating only potatoes from that day onwards. As if God has no other duty than to enter that person's dream to convey how to cook Potato!  Such people are not able to distinguish between reality and the dream because of the power of illusive-reality. These illusions are obstacles on the path of yoga because they cause the practitioner to believe in false realities rather than absolute reality. *Practicing the art of using the power of discrimination (Buddhi) and sticking to reality can help us avoid the traps of illusions set forth by nature. Stories of beautiful damsels tempting sages while they are under extreme-Tapas in the purāṇās are related to this aspect of Bhrānti-Darśana.*

8. **alabdahūmikatva (inability to achieve solid ground):** Consider the following scenario: We are using a treasure map to dig for a diamond box. We are almost there - 99%. At that moment, we feel that we have been wasting our time and start to doubt the map itself. This is because we have not yet achieved a firm foundation in our pursuit. Although our pursuit has brought us 99% closer to the diamond box, a

slight setback has caused us to lose not only the box but also all of our hard work. This is an obstacle because focusing on the end goal and delaying its achievement can lead to discouragement and distort the enthusiasm with which we began. *The way to avoid this obstacle is to focus only on the process of our yoga practice and not on the end goal. As long as our process aligns with our guru's instructions and our attitude is one of discipline, devotion, and dedication, we will have a firm foundation in our intent to pursue the path of yoga.* **Master E K always says, "Yoga is not an achievement, it is an attitude."**

9. **anavasthitatvāni (nature of instability):** An individual may begin with the path of Yoga as taught by Patanjali. Their interest may then grow in Haṭha Yoga, and they may begin to practice some of its techniques. They may then become interested in another path of Yoga. Such erratic movements from one path to another without having a firm foundation in one's beliefs is known as "anavasthi tatvam" This is an obstacle because it breaks the continuity of purpose. When the continuity is broken, the aspirant returns to square one. All of the progress that has been made is lost. *To avoid such obstacles, one must stick to one path and focus their thoughts on the*

*prescribed timetable. The practices should become habitual rather than mechanical. Only a consistent approach will lead to success in the path of Yoga.*

According to Patañjali, these nine impediments are the avoidable obstacles on the path of Yoga. If one succumbs to them, they will lead to weavering of mind (citta-vikṣepa) on the path of Yoga and impede any small amount of success (citta-vṛtti-nirodha) that would have been achieved otherwise. Therefore, it is best to aim to remove these obstacles and tread freely and smoothly.

**Obstacles that are preordained:**

1.  **duḥkha (sorrow):** There are certain situations, such as unfortunate domestic circumstances or the death of a loved one, that can cause emotional distress and lead us astray from the path of yoga. While we cannot control these circumstances, *we can manage our state of mind by learning to accept the reality of life and regularly studying the life stories and teachings of great saints.*

2.  **daurmanasya (mental depression):** If a business associate cheats and steals all the profits, we may feel cheated, used, and taken advantage of. This can

lead to mental depression. We can avoid this by developing a strong will to not let external agents dictate our happiness. Instead of crying after a loss, we should focus on protecting our valued assets. *A firm belief in God and on one's own talent will help them to shield their emotions even in the face of failure.* Such an attitude will help us to overcome the depressed state and continue in the path of Yoga.

3. **aṅgamejayatva (instability of bodily parts):** When we sit for 15 min in Vajrāsana on ground, our feet get numb. Instead if we sit comfortably for meditation on a chair, our buttocks get numb after a while and we would like to get up and then sit again. Holding a particular mudra for a pūja or worship makes hands and fingers painful. Such a shaky state of bodily parts is called Aṅgamejayatva. This is definitely a hurdle for those who would like to sit calmly at a place for some time at least some time a day in order to contemplate on SELF. Hence it is an obstacle for Yogic lifestyle. It is not intended by us, it is what we have been given through our bodily instruments (based on past Karma we acquire our body). *But we do have a way to escape this obstacle. A good healthy diet, Āyurvedic practices such as regular sesame oil massage for the body - oil-pooling - sun-bathing, etc.,long morning and evening walks, good practice of*

*exercises (Sūrya Namaskāras, Sarvāṅgāsana, Śīrṣāsana, etc.), will remove the negative aspects of our bodily instrument and strengthen its stability.*

4. **śvāsa-praśvāsa (inhalation & exhalation):** Respiration can sometimes become a barrier to practicing yoga. Living in a polluted city can reduce the lungs' ability to take in oxygen, which can impede the flow of prāṇa-śakti throughout the body. Additionally, some people are born with breathing problems, such as asthma, which can make breathing exercises prescribed by some yoga schools difficult. This is what Patanjali is pointing out: that even respiration can be a problem in some cases. *One way to overcome respiratory obstacles is to follow medical systems that can strengthen the lungs and avoid triggering medical issues for such patients. Additionally, we can see many saints who achieved sainthood despite having various physical ailments, solely due to their strong will to continue pursuing their ideals, love for humanity, and grace of God. Therefore, if one cultivates these qualities, even respiratory problems will not be an obstacle to practicing yoga.*

In addition to the first nine obstacles, Patañjali states that the next four are also present and impede progress on the path of Yoga. **Vikṣepa+Saḥ+Bhuvaḥ** means "...**are also born along with them causing alterations to the mind...**". In stating that they are also "born", he implies that the later four obstacles manifest during our practice without our intent. But the former nine are definitely due to our own intended misdoings. We must be careful and give our best in escaping each one of these obstacles if at all we hope to achieve the ultimate goal of Yoga one day!

# 32. तत्प्रतिषेधार्थमेकतत्त्वाभ्यासः

## *tat-pratiṣedhārtham-ekatattvābhyāsaḥ*

tat = *that (obstacles);* pratiṣedha = *removal;* artham = *for the sake of;* eka+tattva = *the concept of oneness;* abhyāsaḥ = *repeatedly practice;*

*In order to remove the aforementioned obstacles, (the best method is to) repeatedly practice the (contemplation of) one-ness.*

Usually when we dine, we are expected to savor the food. But our mind reminds us of office work. When we are at work, nearing lunch time, our mind keeps asking us to go to the cafeteria for a pizza. This is a non-yogic state. But in the beginning stages of Yoga, while at dining, mind is on the paneer on plate and while at office work, mind is on the work at hand. In the advanced stages of Yoga, no matter where we are, the mind is only on the ONE that exists through all. This is called EKA-Tattava = the concept of Oneness. As most of us are still in the beginning stages of Yoga, for now we can take the meaning of oneness to be: one-pointed alertness while we are at a particular task.

Such a concept of oneness when practiced helps to overcome all the obstacles. How so? If we closely observe the obstacles which are pre-ordained or the obstacles that are intended by our misdoings, both have their effect only when the mind is "open" to their influence. A stomach pain or a state of sorrow vanishes in sleep. This is because there is no "mind" to feel pain until it has been awakened. In a similar vein, when the mind is fully concentrated on the task at hand, it is unable to pay attention to the obstacles in the way, and therefore, the obstacles are no longer able to impede our progress. By adopting this single-minded focus on the tasks we perform, we will be able to overcome any obstacle.

## 33. मैत्रीकरुणामुदितोपेक्षाणां सुखदुःखपुण्यापुण्य-विषयाणां भावनातश्चित्तप्रसादनम्

**maitrī-karuṇā-mudita-upekṣāṇām-sukha-duḥk**

**ha-puṇya-apuṇya**

**viṣayāṇāṃ-bhāvanātaḥ-citta-prasādanam**

maitrī = *friendship;* karuṇa = *compassion;* mudita = *delight;* upekṣāṇāṃ = *disdain;* sukha+duḥkhaḥ = *happy and sad;* puṇya+apuṇya = *virtuous and sinful;* viṣayāṇāṃ = *things;* bhāvanātaḥ = *thinking resonantly;* citta+prasādanam = *the (monkey) mind is tamed.*

*To help overcome previously mentioned obstacles, consider adopting the following mindset: Cultivate friendships with joyful individuals (as their positive energy can uplift and inspire you), Practice compassion towards those who are less fortunate (as it fosters a sense of empathy and connection), Find delight in the virtuous actions of others (as it reinforces your belief in goodness), Reject and avoid sinful behavior, as it can lead one astray from their path of personal growth. By adopting this mindset, one can create a more positive and supportive environment for themselves, which can help overcome obstacles and achieve the goals.*

## 34. प्रच्छर्दनविधारणाभ्यां वा प्राणस्य

## pracchardhana vidhāraṇābhyāṃ vā prāṇasya

prachchhardhana = *exhalation (and inhalation);* vidhāraṇābhyām = *stillness;* vā = *or;* prāṇasya = *of prāṇa (root pulsation);*

*Or, one can tame the mind by observing the exhalation, inhalation and stillness of prāṇa (root pulsation).*

## 35. विषयवती वा प्रवृत्तिरुत्पन्ना मनसः स्थितिनिबन्धिनी

## viṣayavatī vā pravṛttirutpannā sthiti nibandhinī

viṣayavatī = *sensual things;* vā = *or;* pravṛttiḥ + utpanna = *the birth of behavior;* sthiti = *stability;* nibandhinī = *that which binds.*

*Or, one can tame the mind by observing the birth of behavior of senses towards the sensual objects which bind the mind.*

## 36. विशोका वा ज्योतिष्मती

## viśokā vā jyotiṣmatī

viśokā = *happiness;* vā = *or;* jyotiṣmatī = *the illumined self;*

*Or, one can tame the mind by meditating upon the light of joy within.*

## 37. वीतरागविषयं वा चित्तम्

## vītarāgaviṣayaṃ vā cittam

vītarāga = *person who mastered detachment;* vā = *or;*

cittaṃ = *the mind of.*

*Or, one can tame the mind by meditating upon the light of joy within.*

## 38. स्वप्न निद्रा ज्ञानालम्बनं वा

## svapna nidrā jñānālambanaṃ vā

svapna = *dream;* nidrā = *sleep;* jñāna + ālambanaṃ = *or*

*taking support in the knowledge of;* vā = *or.*

*Or, one can tame the mind by taking support in the process of knowing what it means to dream and what it means to enter into sleep.*

## 39. यथाभिमतध्यानाद्वा

## yathābhimata dhyānādvā

yathābhimata = *as per one's school of thought;* dhyānāt =

*meditate;* vā = *or.*

*Or, one can tame the mind by meditating as per our own school of thought.*

<u>**Positive reinforcement:**</u> Our current task is to overcome the obstacles in our path. The solution lies in contemplating the

unity of all things. However, when we attempt to begin this practice, various distractions may lead us astray. This is especially true at the critical juncture where the mind interacts with the world. It is important to remember that every aspect of existence has both positive and negative facets, much like the two sides of a coin. In this sutra, Patañjali provides four examples and indirectly encourages us to adopt a positive mindset towards everything or, at the very least, a neutral and non-reactive disposition.

In our daily interactions, we encounter individuals who exude a remarkable capacity for unconditional happiness. By closely observing them and fostering friendships (maitrī) with them, we can attune ourselves to this delightful state of mind. Friendship has the inherent ability to subtly blend aspects of our friend's character into our own. Therefore, it is essential to cultivate friendships with those who derive their happiness not from material possessions but from an inner sense of well-being. By doing so, we can instill a sense of calmness and tranquility within our open minds.

Conversely, we also encounter individuals who are inexplicably miserable for reasons unknown to us. We might assume that we would be happier in their circumstances, yet they remain perpetually unhappy and sorrowful. After reading the preceding suggestion, one might hastily conclude that we should avoid befriending such people. However, this notion is erroneous. Patañjali gently urges us to cultivate compassion (karuṇā) towards them. This approach not only prevents the development of hatred or other negative emotions within us but also reinforces our fundamental human nature. It prepares us to readily offer assistance should they require it.

Amidst the worthy, a few stand out as exceptionally virtuous. Their positive character is so powerful that their presence and actions evoke a sense of warmth within us. It is essential to cultivate a feeling of delight (muditā) towards such individuals. By taking pleasure in their conduct, we are inspired to emulate their actions and thoughts. This emulation gradually transforms us, making us more virtuous as well.

On the contrary, we might encounter individuals whose actions and plans consistently trouble others. Instead of harboring hatred towards them, Patañjali advises us to practice willful ignorance (upekṣā). This approach is recommended during the initial stages of Yoga, when our minds are yet to be trained. Engaging in opposition against such misdeeds can pollute the mind with added complexities. However, this does not imply that we should neglect the defense of good against evil. Rather, we must uphold righteousness without becoming attached emotionally to the notion of eliminating evil.

By instilling positive qualities into the thought processes of the numerous pairs of opposites in the world, we can tame the mind. This is the process of Citta-Prasādanam. It is the initial step towards cittavṛtti nirodha, the cessation of mental fluctuations. It is imperative to acknowledge the substantial importance of this sūtra and refrain from treating it as a mere footnote. For this sūtra serves as the essential groundwork for managing the restless mind and ultimately aspiring to eradicate its various transformations.

**<u>(Or) Observe the respiration</u>**: The foundation of our life is built upon the processes of inhalation and exhalation. These actions are the effects of primary pulsation, which is referred to as Prāṇa, the life force. Observing the breath as it enters and exits the body has a calming effect on the mind, which is naturally linked to the breath. It is common for individuals to advise tense people to "take a deep breath" in order to calm their agitated minds. When the mind becomes calm through observing the cycles of respiration, a state of stillness in the breath is achieved. This stillness is not a deliberate act of holding the breath, but rather a natural stillness of prāṇic activity. Prāṇa only exerts itself when necessary, and this necessity arises when the mind is active and demands more life force. In deep sleep (when the mind is dissolved), we sometimes observe that the breath may stop (for a few seconds) or become very slow. Prāṇa does not waste itself unnecessarily unless compelled by the mind.

Patañjali proposes an alternative approach to breath control, suggesting that instead of employing forceful techniques like measured inhalation, exhalation, and breath retention, one should focus on observing the natural respiration and its source. This practice will induce stillness in the life force (prāṇa), leading to a calming effect on the mind. Patañjali elaborates on this concept in the subsequent chapter, referring to it as prāṇāyāma.

**(Or) Use the sensual objects:** Initially, during the early stages of Yoga, we predominantly reside within the physical realm, bounded by experiences obtained through our senses as we interact with sensual objects. This state is referred to as "Viṣayavatī." Although initially this may appear undesirable, we can use it to our advantage.

Consider the contrasting effects of placing a rotten object versus a sweet-smelling flower in our room. The former induces agitation, while the latter brings us solace. When we become attached to an object, its absence can cause renewed agitation the following day.

Therefore, sense objects have the capacity to either bind us or soothe us, depending on our level of intimacy with them. By gradually practicing Vairāgya (non-attachment), we can effectively eliminate our habit of attachment. Furthermore, we can harness the soothing element by incorporating an abundance of similar pleasant things into our lives to help calm the mind.

For instance, we can decorate our home with soft, smooth-textured fabrics, sweet-smelling camphor, and colorful flowers. These elements are especially beneficial when used in a worship room, as they expedite the devotional process. This method is recommended by the elders in the Āgama Śāstrās for worship.

As the mind finds tranquility in the presence of harmonious sense objects, Patañjali takes us a step further. He encourages us to observe the origin of our reactions to the environment. Where does this sense of like or dislike for certain objects arise from? As the mind relishes in the presence of the selected objects, it becomes receptive to our suggestive method. This gradual process culminates in a state of profound stillness, known as Citta-prasādanam.

**<u>(Or) Meditate on the light of joy within:</u>** In the previous technique, we learned that sensual objects can help calm the mind's disturbances, and we were advised to focus on the origin of sensual reactions. From a scientific perspective, all sensory inputs are transmitted to the brain as electrical currents through the nerves, and the brain responds accordingly. However, what distinguishes one electrical current from another in the brain? According to present scientific understanding, there is no qualitative difference between nerve currents, only quantitative differences in their magnitude of amperes/volts. So how do we perceive the rich diversity of the experiential world?

There is an inherent spiritual light that emanates from the Self, illuminating the corresponding areas of the brain and facilitating the processing of information. This same light is also responsible for generating thoughts, even when they are not connected to sensory objects. For instance, when we are hungry, simply imagining a banana can cause our mouths to water. This is known as "Jyotishmati," or the Light of the Mind. By retracing the path of meditation from physical objects, through the senses, and beyond the mind, we enter the realm of this abundant light.

In this sūtra, Patañjali instructs us to meditate on this light, whose natural state is "Ānanda" (bliss) or "Viśokā" (freedom from sorrow). This practice will lead us to calming the mind, as this light is the source and power of the mind.

*Note: The principle of "As above, so below" (yat piṇḍe tat brahmāṇḍe) can also be used in meditation to internalize external light. The sunrise or sunset colors are optimal choices because they are directly linked to the awakening and dissolving aspects of consciousness. This is why the practice of Sandhya Vandana (worship of the sun at twilight) is prescribed for those following the solar path. Additionally, astrological science (Jyotirvidya) can be used to determine the best colors for inducing calmness, and these colors can then be incorporated into one's daily environment. The root principle of color therapy is based on this sūtra.*

**(Or) Learn from the detached:** If we observe those around us, we will notice individuals who are completely absorbed in the world's affairs, while others are entirely detached. However, it's essential to clarify that detached individuals are not those who have merely abandoned their responsibilities. In this context, Vitarāgas refers to individuals who fulfill their duties without becoming entangled in the dualities of life events.

Patanjali encourages us to observe such individuals, learn from them, and meditate on how their minds have achieved such a state. By contemplating the qualities of these pious, detached people, we can induce our own minds into the Vitarāga stage through self-suggestion. It's worth noting that the mind only reacts when it experiences the dualities of good and bad, among others. In a Vitarāga state, these dualities cease to exist, leaving the mind with no scope to react. Consequently, the mind exists in its own natural state, which is the Self. This state of calmness can be achieved by meditating on the qualities of such pious detached individuals.

**(Or) Understand the states of dream & sleep:** Each day, we experience sleep, wakefulness and dreaming. These states are as natural as any others in our lives. If we meditate on them properly, they can serve as powerful tools for unlocking the mysteries of our existence. However, it is common knowledge that we have no control over our minds when we are asleep. We cannot construct or navigate our dreams, nor can we voluntarily enter or exit sleep. We simply lie down and sleep takes over. Even when an alarm is ringing, we wake up only when we wake up - there is no other way. So how can we heed Patanjali's advice to meditate on sleep and dreams, when our sense of self disappears in these states?

The suggestion can be understood as "try to meditate". Each night before sleep, we should attempt to observe ourselves as we fall asleep. This should be done without agitation or concentration - just passive observation. As we practice this over time, we will gradually learn the art of conscious sleeping. This will allow us to begin meditating on how dreams arise and eventually, to consciously dream. In doing so, our minds will automatically achieve tranquility.

This is because they will have learned how to dissolve at will, while still retaining a part of themselves to enjoy those states.

**(Or) One's own school of thought:** If none of the above works for an aspirant, Patañjali here offers complete freedom of approach in regards to taming the mind. He says that one can follow their own methodology (of course having obtained thorough practical knowledge from a guru or an experienced Yogi) which will also calm the mind, because it would have been a time-tested method.

Some of the methods include the following:
- Listening to or participating in devotional singing
- Sitting dedicatedly in the discourses of Rāmāyaṇa, Mahābhārata, etc.
- Painting the nature or poetically describing the nature
- Practicing the art of service to fellow human in need
- etc.

In this way whatever be the method applied, it is the dedication and sincerity that makes the mind calm!

## 40. परमाणु परममहत्त्वान्तोऽस्य वशीकारः

## pramāṇu parama mahattvāntoṣsya vaśīkāraḥ

paramāṇu = *the smallest of the small;* parama + mahattva = *the largest of the large;* antaḥ = *up to the end;* asya = *for the yoga-practitioner;* vaśīkāraḥ = *mastery over mind is achieved;*

*For the practitioner of yoga, taming of the mind results in mastery over its capacity to meditate on the smallest of the small (atom) as well as the largest of the large.*

Through the successful taming of the mind, as previously mentioned, an individual gains the ability to comprehend the Universe from the smallest atoms to the vastness of the cosmos. This understanding is possible because our minds are inextricably linked to the broader mind of the Universe.

Imagine an iceberg floating in water, seemingly separate but formed from the same water. When the iceberg melts, it becomes indistinguishable from the water. Similarly, when our minds maintain their individuality, marked by persistent alterations, we cannot grasp our place in the Universe and become entangled in life's events. However, when the mind becomes absolutely calm, it dissolves into the Universal mind, transcending its perceived individuality.

"Paramāṇu" also represents the tiny existence of the individual within the vast Universe. In contrast, "Parama Mahattva" signifies the individual's universal existence, encompassing the vast cosmos. The yoga journey begins at the atomic state and culminates in the Universal state, undertaken voluntarily by the Yogi (through willpower) and facilitated by the newly trained mind due to the acquired power of "vaśīkāra."

**41.** क्षीणवृत्तेरभिजातस्येव मणेर्ग्रहीतृ

ग्रहणग्राह्येषु तत्स्थतदञ्जनता समापत्तिः

**kṣīṇavṛtte rabhijātasyeva maṇergṛhītṛ grahaṇa**

**grāhyeṣutatstha tadañjanatā samāpattiḥ**

kṣīṇavṛtteḥ = *when the alterations of the mind reduce;* abhijātasya = *that belonging to superior quality;* maṇeḥ = *crystal;* iva = *just like;* grahīta = *the one who perceives;* grahaṇa = *the process of perception;* grāhyeṣu = *the one that is perceived;* tatstha = *in that resides;* tadañjanatā = *adherence (of color);* samāpattiḥ = *is samāpatti.*

*As we progress through the earlier stages of mind-taming and cittavṛtti nirodha gradually unfolds, we transition into a realm known as Samāpatti. To grasp this concept, visualize a pristine crystal that appears to mirror the hues of its surroundings. While it may seem to blend in, the crystal's essence remains unaltered. This untouched stage of consciousness is Samāpatti (a stage before samādhi).*

**42.** तत्र शब्दार्थज्ञानविकल्पैः संकीर्णा सवितर्का समापत्तिः

**tatra śabdārtha jñāna vikalpaiḥ**

## saṃkīrṇā savitarka samāpattiḥ

tatra = *there;* śabdārtha = *the meaning of the word;* jñāna = *true knowledge;* vikalpaiḥ = *different modifications;* saṃkīrṇā = *mixed;* savitarka samāpattiḥ = *samāpatti by awareness.*

*The first type of Samāpatti is the untouched stage of consciousness where awareness is intact and responds to the mixed stimuli of the external sound (or color or shape or number) and through that chaos, acquires calmness. This is called Savitarka Samāpatti (a stage before samādhi).*

## 43. स्मृतिपरिशुद्धौ स्वरूपशून्येवार्थमात्रनिर्भासा निर्वितर्का
## smṛti pariśuddhau svarūpa śūnyeva
## arthamātra nirbhāsā nirvitarkā

smṛti = *there;* pariśuddhau = *cleansed of;* svarūpa = *self-form;* śūnya+iva = *vanish;* arthamātra = *essence;* nirbhāsā = *radiate;* nirvitarkā = *samāpatti by absence of awareness.*

*In the second type of Samāpatti, the mind is cleansed of all recollections, causing the forms to vanish, leaving only the essence to radiate.*

As we embark on the journey of taming the mind, gradually attaining cittavṛtti nirodha, we transition into a stage known as Samāpatti. Imagine a pristine crystal, suspended in the air, its facets reflecting the kaleidoscope of colors that dance around it. While it may seem to blend seamlessly with its surroundings, the crystal's essence remains unaltered, untouched by the colors that envelop it. This state of intertwined and yet untouched consciousness is the essence of Samāpatti. This Samāpatti is a profound stage where the mind basically becomes like a mirror, reflecting the world around it without judgment or attachment.

Samāpatti serves as a foreground for the state of Samādhi that we shall soon delve into. It offers us a pre-taste of what a Samādhi stage feels like. As such, it is an indispensable prerequisite that must be attained before one can embark on the journey towards Samādhi.

In that there are two kinds of Samāpatti
- **Savitarka Samāpatti** - stage of consciousness attained via internal harmonious response to external chaotic stimuli.
- **Nirvitarka Samāpatti** - stage of consciousness attained via essential internal silence.

**Savitarka Samāpatti**

To think that Savitarka is lower in nature and Nirvitarka is higher in nature is like to think the head of a coin is glorious than the tail of a coin. Savitarka means Sa + Vitarka =

including the logic of various things. Let us take the example of Sage Nārada, who is one of the greatest sages ever existing in the whole hierarchy of descendants of God's divine emanations. When the name of "Śrī Harī" is uttered, he just goes into ecstasy of experiencing Lord Nārāyaṇa. Same with lord Hanumān, the moment the name of "Śrī Rāma" is heard, he goes into the sublime state of Samādhi!

This stage that is pushing one into internal ecstasy by the mixed stimuli of external SOUND is called "Savitarka" Samāpatti. Pataṇjali is suggesting that in the journey to Samādhi, there comes a stage where we train to see harmony in seeming mixed chaos. This harmonious view comes when detachment and reflection as mentioned earlier establishes in the mind, but at first by conscious awareness.. In such harmony, the knowledge of the sound (or color or shape or number) reveals not the qualities or quantities of the object but only reveals the essence of the object. For instance, we arrange our room for worship, light the incense sticks and dīpa, decorate the Lord's pictures with flowers, etc. This helps in arranging the inner mind into beautiful harmony. Instead of forcing it into samādhi, the mind just slides into samādhi. Therefore, to attain Samāpatti is not the goal, but to retain it by ever practicing the "attitude of Yogic life" is the most important point to be understood from Patañjali's instructions.

One example can be - imagine we are being spoken to by our friend. Before the stage of embarking upon Yoga, we see them as our friend and associated character obtained from processing our memories upto that time of interaction. But in the path of Yoga, when we reach the stage of Samāpatti, we reflect the friend's presence without getting tainted by the nature of the friend. When the friend speaks, even though the sounds are of mixed nature (the tone and intention) we will start to hear what he/she needs rather than to what he/she wants. Why? because, we have become so calm that we can see clearly through the stable reality from the mixed reality and hence can aid them in a real sense of the word "help". But the only thing here is that we know we are observing, we are helping, ..... the sense of "we" exists how much ever dim it may be. This is conscious-awareness and is called Savitarka-samāpatti.

**Nirvitarka Samāpatti**

Upon mastering Savitarka Samāpatti, the Yoga-student transitions into a unique stage. Previously, they believed their actions and responses were driven by their benevolence, shaping the prosperity of society. This "I am" sense fosters conscious awareness. However, in Nirvitarka Samāpatti, the "I am" dissolves, reflecting the universal "I AM". Doership, ownership, and all else fade into a serene experience of silence—a silence devoid of sound, number, color, and shape. While the person in Nirvitarka still recognizes these elements, there is no "person" in the conventional sense. Individuality gives way to Universality. The external chaos and the Savitarka Samāpatti's response to it are now inverted. There's no external or internal, only universal rhythm. Similar to a mathematician perceiving rhythmic patterns in randomness, Nirvitarka reveals a gentle silence permeating all realms.

In the example of the friend, the Savitarka person begins to see the needs of their friend and can therefore offer help accordingly. However, a person in Nirvitarka sees neither the friend nor themselves, but only the pure bond of friendship. This bond is seen as an emanation of God's pure love. This allows them to become an instrument of God, helping the friend only in accordance with the divine plan without any interference from their ego. Although this is challenging to explain, a Savitarka person can enter into the Nirvitarka stage by simply practicing the integration of their personal ego into Universal oneness. This is referred to as "Smṛti Pariśuddhau" - the cleansing of the memory, where personal associations are dissolved into purposeful actions. This is the best place to relate "Īśvara praṇidhānāt" concept. Submission to GOD - Almighty. In Savitarka, the submission happens to their defined GOD whereas in Nirvitarka the definition of GOD loses its base which is replaced by the pure unified experience (not separate awareness unlike in savitarka). This is the state from where Mahāvākyās have been uttered forth by the greatest seers of ancient lore, which are enumerated below:

- *Tvam Asi* (तत् त्वम् असि) - I AM THAT
- *Ahaṁ Brahmāsmi* (अहं ब्रह्मास्मि) - I AM BRAHMAN
- *Prajñānaṁ Brahma* (प्रज्ञानं ब्रह्म) - BRAHMAN IS CONSCIOUSNESS
- *Ayam Ātmā Brahma* (अयम् आत्मा ब्रह्म) - THIS SOUL IS BRAHMAN
- *Sarvaṃ Khalvidaṃ Brahma* - EVERYTHING IS BRAHMAN

*The journey of the Yogi is the story contained in the pages between the first page — "I am" — and the last page — "THAT/BRAHMAN," — in the book of life. The concept of OM (tasya vācakaḥ praṇavaḥ) and God-submission (īśvara praṇidhānā) are the essence of the book itself, and Savitarka and Nirvitarka are the final chapters.*

## 44. एतैव सविचारा निर्विचारा च सूक्ष्मविषया व्याख्याता

## etaiva savicārā nirvicārā ca

## sūkṣmaviṣayā vyākhyātā

etaiva = *by this only;* savicārā = *stage including awareness* nirvicārā = *stage not including awareness;* ca = *and;* sūkṣma+viṣayā = *having subtlety;* vyākhyātā = *has been explained.*

*By this only (the previous aphorisms) we have also explained what is otherwise known as Savicārā (same as savitarka) and Nirvicārā (same as nirvitarka) stages .*

When a student is enthusiastic and eager in their pursuit of knowledge, it's natural for them to explore multiple resources beyond what has been prescribed by their Guru or teacher. This inquisitiveness can lead to a deeper understanding, but it can also create confusion.

Patañjali, recognizing this tendency, offers further clarification to prevent misunderstanding. He explains that the previously mentioned stages of Savitarka and Nirvitarka Samadhi are also known as Savicara and Nirvicāra Samadhi, respectively. That is why he says "Eta Eva = by what has been said before".

The terms "Vitarka" and "Vicara" both relate to the act of thinking or reasoning.

- **Savitarka and Savicara Samāpatti** represent the initial stage before Samadhi, where awareness is still present. In these stages, the practitioner is actively engaged in contemplation and analysis, using their intellect to understand the object of meditation.

- **Nirvitarka and Nirvicara Samāpatti** represent the advanced stage before Samadhi, where individual awareness dissolves. In these stages, the mind transcends thought and reasoning, merging with the object of meditation in a state of pure consciousness.

Patanjali's clarification is crucial for preventing confusion among students. Without this guidance, the curious student might become lost in intellectual analysis, forgetting the ultimate goal of Samadhi, which is the synthesis of the individual consciousness with the universal consciousness.

The practice of Samadhi is a journey from the analytical mind to the intuitive mind. It involves a gradual shift from thinking about reality to directly experiencing reality. By understanding the different stages of Samadhi and the subtle distinctions between them, the student can navigate this journey with greater clarity and avoid the pitfalls of intellectualization.

## 45. सूक्ष्मविषयत्वं चालिङ्गपर्यवसानम्

## sūkṣma viṣayatvam ca aliñga paryavasānam

**sūkṣhma** = *very subtle;* **viṣayatvam** = *essence;* **ca** = *and;* **a+liṅga** = *having no symbol;* **paryavasānam** = *is the result.*

*This path leads to (understanding of) the subtle things (the true subjective light behind the objective world). This happens along with a total annihilation of the symbolic world.*

Our world consists of both material and non-material elements. The non-material self comprehends the material world through the mind, which acts as an interface. This understanding typically involves modifications and alterations of the mind (citta-vṛtti). When these alterations are not nullified, everything becomes a symbolic representation of understanding.

Let's take a scenic view as an example. In reality, it is just energy manifested in different forms of matter. When sunlight interacts with this matter, it scatters. However, when this scattered light interacts with our visual system, it creates a sense of beauty. Instead of recognizing the energy and light as the source of beauty, we focus on the sensation and exclaim "Wow, what a scenery!". We even believe this to be true and share our experiences with friends. This is the result of Citta-Vṛtti, or ripples on the mind's surface. The feeling of beauty we have is based on the symbol of what is perceived by the eye and interpreted by the mind.

This concept applies to all interactions, whether awake or dreaming. A SYMBOL represents the foundation upon which we understand an entity's existence. All physical forms, relationships, and perceptions rely on symbols, known in scriptures as "LIṄGA." Going into scriptures, the word "Liṅga Śarīra" refers to the symbol or support underlying the physical body, also called the astral body or vehicle of consciousness. Similar to how iron dust gathers around magnetic field lines, revealing their existence, physical matter gathers around the liṅga śarīra, shaping the body and indicating the presence of the soul. In purāṇās, the term "Śiva Liṅga" attributes an oval shape to the formless god, providing a conceptual support to comprehend the formless infinity.

The term LIṄGA refers to a symbol or framework that shapes our understanding and perception. When someone achieves Savitarka or Savicāra samāpatti, their awareness remains. This means they depend on symbols for interpretation and response. The difference between a yogi in the early stages and one in this stage is that the latter's responses are more refined and stem from inner peace.

However, relying on symbolic understanding of the world indicates that they haven't yet penetrated the illusion to perceive the underlying reality.

However, when one enters Nirvitarka or Nirvicāra stage, the symbols dissolve. This occurs because symbols only function when there's both an external source pole and an internal receiving pole. As scriptures state, this internal receiver is the Liṅga Śarīra, which houses impressions from past lives and reacts to external stimuli. The astral body remains whole in the Savitarka stage. However, it begins to disintegrate as one moves into the Nirvitarka stage, marking the start of the dissolution of symbols. Without a receiving pole, there is no interpretation of the transmission from the transmitting pole - the surrounding world.

In the Nirvitarka stage, a Yogi begins to comprehend the true nature of reality, transcending mere appearances. Patanjali refers to this as "Sūkṣma Viṣayatvam," where only the essence of things is perceived. In this stage, all forms of differentiation ("LIṄGA") cease to exist, a stage Patanjali calls "A-LIṄGA." These two stages occur simultaneously, akin to how light enters a room when a window is opened, dispelling the darkness immediately.

## 46. ता एव सबीज समाधिः

## tā eva sabīja samādhiḥ

tā = *those;* eva = *(are) only;* sa + bīja = *with seed;* samādhiḥ = *samādhiḥ.*

**The aforementioned are stages of Samādhi with seed.**

The highest aim of Yoga is to reach Samādhi, which is the only natural state of being. Our current state, before practicing Yoga, is artificial. Samādhi is pure and shouldn't be described by any other words. However, on the path to Samādhi, there are finer stages that can be considered part of the overall Samādhi experience. These distinctions are only to help practitioners understand their progress and stay focused on the ultimate goal, not for self-glorification.

Patañjali previously referred to Samāpati as Savitarka/Savicāra and Nirvitarka/Nirvicāra. He now states that these are actually graded stages in attaining Samādhi containing bīja, or seeds.

The nature of this concept of "seed" is explained now.

Consider the following example: Chickpeas, when stored in a jar, appear dry and lifeless, with no apparent potential for growth. However, if you soak and wrap them in a cloth, they will sprout within a few days. This shows that our initial perception of the chickpeas as lifeless was wrong. Although they seemed dormant, they possessed a hidden potential for life. Due to the subtle nature of this potential, only time can reveal it. This illustrates that even when something appears lifeless, it may not actually be so.

This germinating principle is called the "Bīja" concept. Due to the cyclicity and periodicity of our soul's incarnations, we would have had collected many a seeds of "Guṇa" or qualities. The whole set of these makes us who we are in our current lives. By living a Yoga-life, one aims to annihilate these Guṇas so that they can be purest of the pure.

Achieving Samāpatti can give the awareness (in Savitarka) or the being itself (in Nirvitarka) a feeling of transcending the qualitative world. They are akin to dried chickpeas on a shelf, seemingly devoid of any future life. However, when provided with the right environment—water and time—chickpeas undoubtedly sprout. Similarly, those stuck in the Samāpatti stage can potentially regress on the ascending ladder of the Yoga path. All it takes is the right environment to trigger this downward slide.

A yogi once visited a village, proclaiming that he had conquered anger. A mischievous young boy, curious to test the yogi's claim, challenged him to eat a chili pepper. The yogi, confident in his self-mastery, accepted the challenge.

As the yogi consumed each chili pepper, the boy continued to provoke him. Finally, after the tenth chili pepper, the burning sensation overwhelmed the yogi's composure, and he angrily shouted at the boy.

Patanjali refers to this as "**Sabīja Samādhi**," emphasizing that the seeds carried over from countless lives remain embedded within us, ready to sprout given the right conditions. Therefore, even the seemingly pure and transcendent stages of Savitarka and Nirvitarka are not exempt from the potential reemergence of past tendencies. The yogi who believed he had conquered his anger was mistaken, as the anger lay dormant, awaiting the right moment to resurface.

****Note:** *Seeds can be prevented from sprouting by dry roasting them. The heat from dry roasting stops the germination process, meaning they won't sprout even after being soaked. Similarly, a yogi who is in "Tapas" is metaphorically "dry roasting" the seeds of their Gunas in the fire of yoga. This "fire of yoga" refers to the three fires of Āhavnīya Agni (intellectual fire), Gārhapatya Agni (digestive fire), and Dakṣiṇa Agni (reproductive fire).*

## 47. निर्विचारवैशारद्येऽध्यात्मप्रसादः

## nirvicāra vaiśāradhye' adhyātma prasādaḥ

nirvicāra = *those in the stage of nirvicāra;* viśāradhya = *gets ultimate mastery (clarity);* adhi + ātma = *that I AM which supports the I am;* prasādaḥ = *will start to shine forth or become evident.*

*When the Yoga sādhaka in the stage of Nirvicāra gains mastery, the true omni-self "I AM" which assumes the form of individual self "I am" will start to shine forth and become trivially evident.*

## 48. ऋतम्भरा तत्र प्रज्ञा

## ṛtambharā tatra prajñā

ṛtambharā = *the embodiment of Eternal Truth;* tatra = *there;* prajña = *higher consciousness.*

*The elevated stage of consciousness attained by such a Yogi is known as Ṛtambharā - The embodiment of Eternal Truth.*

## 49. श्रुतानुमानप्रज्ञाभ्यामन्यविषया विशेषार्थत्वात्

## śrutānumāna prajñābhyām

## anyaviṣayā viśeṣārthatvāt

śruta = *that which is heard;* anumāna = *indirect inference;* prajñābyām = *consciousness (in previous two states);* anyaviṣayā = *other things;* viśeṣa + arthatvāt = *gives a different and unique understanding.*

*The understanding of consciousness that a yogi attains through the Ṛtambharā prajña will be distinct and unique compared to the understanding gained through either direct experience (sensory perception) or indirect inference (intellectual and scriptural).*

## 50. तज्जः संस्कारोऽन्यसंस्कारप्रतिबन्धी

## tajjaḥ saṃskāro anya saṃskāra pratibandhī

tat+jaḥ = *born out of that state;* saṃskāraḥ = *behavioral spontaneity;* anya + saṃskāraḥ = *other erruptions;* prati + bandhī = *will block.*

*The (purest) behavioral spontaneity which is born out of the Ṛtambharā state will prevent any further eruptions (from the ocean of the mind).*

## 51. तस्यापि निरोधे सर्वनिरोधान्निर्बीजः समाधिः

## tasyāpi nirodhe sarvanirodhānnirbījaḥ samādhiḥ

tasya+api = *that also;* nirodhe = *having halted;* sarva + nirodhāt = *everything else is halted;* niḥ + bījaḥ + samādhiḥ = *attainment having no seed.*

*Only when that (purest behavioral spontaneity) is halted everything else (opinions or ideas etc) will be halted or cease to exist. That stage of consciousness is called SEEDLESS-ATTAINMENT - Nirbīja Samādhi.*

Patañjali previously cautioned that our current stage, samādhi, still contains seeds of personal impressions. Regardless of the depth of silence we attain, it can be undone in a single moment. To prevent this and achieve the ultimate goal, it is advised to first attain mastery over the Nirvicāra stage.

When we are in a state of Nirvicara, we are without reflective thoughts. Reflection is a property of the mind; we reflect when we have a mind of our own. According to Patanjali, the mind is its vritties. In the Nirvicara state, the mind and its vritties are slowly dissolved, and reflection ceases. When we greet a friend, we live in that moment without reflection or projection of thought into the past or future. We don't greet them because they have helped us in the past or because they may help us in the future. We greet them simply because we greet them - there is no other reason except to be part of the divine play! Our smile should radiate pure love (without expectations). Our responses to them should be what they need to hear, rather than what we want to say (because we have no wants). This is the outcome of mastering the Nirvicara state. The self loses its grip on its own projections and begins to merge with the background consciousness. The true "I AM" will start to radiate in place of the false "I am". This is akin to clearing of the mud from the water revealing diamonds in its depths. This is what the word "Prasāda" exactly means in this context. Adhi+Ātma+Prasāda = that true self which has been supporting the very existence will start to shine forth.

The Vedas define Ṛtam as the eternal truth that rhythmically governs the laws of the universe. This differs from Satyam, which refers to the truths that manifest as individual expressions of beings within the universe and are derived from those universal laws. For instance, the statement "The sun rises in the east" is an example of Ṛtam as it is based on universal laws, whereas the statement "I ate a banana" is dependent on individual experience and thus an example of Satyam. When our consciousness ascends to the Ṛtambharā Prajña stage, we gain a deeper understanding of this eternal truth.

The consciousness traversing from Citta-Vṛtties (mental modifications) to Samprajñāta & Asamprajñāta (detachments) to Savitarka & Nirvitarka Samāpatti (untouched stages of consciousness) will now enter into penultimate stage of Ṛtambharā Prajña. Consciousness merges and thus becomes the eternal truth that governs the entire Universe - The LAW of the Universe itself. This stage is inexplicable. Up to this stage, consciousness relied upon the bodily instruments be it five senses or the mind to understand the Universe in and around. But now, it attained the grand status of ṚTAM - the eternal throb of LIFE itself, it is unique and incomparable to any of the previous experiences or understandings it had.

Also, Patañjali states "viśeṣa arthavāt". Śeṣa means that which has a remainder and "vi+śeṣa" means that which has no remainder. Prior to this stage, consciousness had only limited understanding of all that it interacted with. The statement itself suggests that consciousness is separate from the things it interacted with and hence there was the interaction. But in Ṛtambharā stage, consciousness merges with the background and thus it doesn't see anything as a separate from it. So there won't be any remainders left when apparent individual consciousness interacts or acts in the drama of creation. It knows and understands every object, every thing, every person, every relation, every law not as a separate entity in the Universe but as a part of a single being (itself as Uni-VERSE). This is what Viśeṣa+arthavāt means.

Let yogi stay and master even the Ṛtambharā stage some more time. Just like churning milk gives butter from this stage emerges a Unique Samskāra which brings a halt to all other samskāras.

Samskāra means behavioral spontaneity. Let us say there are two children playing. When a class teacher suddenly approaches them, one still plays around while the other stops and greets "Hari Om" to the teacher and may also seek blessings by offering a namaskara mudra. Similarly, when someone is in need of immediate help, a person may seek to escape the situation while the other may readily jump in to offer the needed help. This spontaneous behaviour stems from what we call in Sanskrit as SAMSKĀRA. So Samskara is defined as a behavioral spontaneity. Usually Samskāra means good samskāra and bad samskāra is termed kusamskāra.

Here Patañjali speaks of Good samskārās. Prior to the stage of Ṛtambharā, the behavior of the Yogi would have transformed from wantful to the needful. But being under the stage of consciousness with seeds, they have a taint of personal impressions in seed form. After mastering the Ṛtambharā stage, slowly like butter coming out of milk, a special samskāra emerges which reveals to the consciousness that ALL IS ONE. This gives a push to the consciousness to enter into the highest realm - The Kingdom of GOD. In that kingdom, there is no more emergence of any idea of their own or an opinion of their own.

Not that ideas wont come, but the ownership of the ideas is totally lost. Behavior of such a person will be similar to the behavior of Lord Sri Krishna as showcased by Bhāgavata and Mahābhārata. He was cunning with Duryodhana, friendly with Arjuna, lovingly with Subhadra, loyal with Gopas and Gopis, etc. He was like a mirror which reflects the light without itself getting affected. So stopping all other samskārās means to stop proposals from emerging within the mind and act. There is no individual mind to propose to be blunt. Only GOD-mindedness exists and this is the reason why everything else is halted by this one unique samskāra that emerged out of Ṛtambharā Prajña.

If a Yogi is even successful to stop this ONE special Samskāra - by grace of GOD - instead of acting similar to the Lord he acts as the Lord! This stage is called nirbīja samādhi - The SEEDLESS ATTAINMENT. If we speak anything else other than this it will become speculation because only a person in samāhi can experience what it is. Even the Yogi in Samādhi is helpless in explaining us it's beauties - because words cannot measure it nor can our mind comprehend it. How can mind - part of a whole - can ever comprehend the WHOLE? Therefore, even Patañjali stops this Samādhi pāda by saying that it is seedless samādhi and does not venture to describe anything else. The onus of experiencing what it is falls on the YOGI.

# About The Author

Dr. Tejaswi Katravulapally is a scholar with a PhD in Quantum Physics (EMJD-EXTATIC scholarship, Ireland & Poland), specializing in ultrafast laser-atom interactions. His academic background also includes an MSc in Physics from IIT Madras and a B.Tech in ECE from LNMIIT, Jaipur. Beyond his scientific pursuits, Dr. Tejaswi is an accomplished Carnatic flautist with over a decade of experience. He is also a published author of five books that delve into Vedic scriptures such as the Suparna Suktam, Purusha Suktam, Lalita Sahasranama, Mandukya Upanishad, and Yoga Sutras.

Growing up in a devout Indian family fostered his early spiritual development, which was further shaped by learning the flute (Nada Yoga) at the age of ten and by his deep connection with his Guru, Master E.K. (Sri Ekkirala Krishnamacharya). He is ever in the study and practice of the Bhagavad Gita, Upanishads, Sri Vidya and other branches of Sanatana Dharma.

Currently, Dr. Tejaswi is a part-time faculty member at Kriya Tantra Institute, USA, where he teaches courses on Tantra and Mantra Sastras. He also serves as an online guest lecturer at LNMIIT, Jaipur, for the UGC-mandated Indian Knowledge System (IKS) course. In recognition of his efforts in propagating IKS, Dr. Tejaswi was honored with the "*Spiritual Scientist*" award in 2024 by the "All India center for local self government," Andhra University.

Dr. Tejaswi is dedicated to integrating Western science and Eastern philosophy, aiming to enhance learning through a synthesis of diverse viewpoints.

Readers can contact the author at ardentdisciple7@gmail.com.

## 1) Lalitā Priyadīpikā: Splendours of the World Mother

*In the ancient wisdom traditions of India (Bhārat), the practice of worshipping the Divine through a thousand names, known as Sahasranāma, has endured through time. The term Sahasranāma combines "Sahasra" (thousand or infinite) and "Nāma" (name). This form of worship involves vocally uttering each name while meditating on its profound significance, with the ultimate aim of dissolving the individual self into the universal Oneness. The splendors of this omniscient Divine are often personified as the World Mother, Lalitā. The Lalitā Sahasranāma comprises a thousand names that encapsulate the diverse qualities of this divine feminine principle, guiding spiritual aspirants toward experiencing the magnificence of the Almighty.*

*The "Lalitā Priyadīpika" series represents a dedicated endeavor to unravel the essence of each of the thousand names found within the original Lalitā Sahasranāma text. This exploration delves into considerable depth, providing word-by-word meanings, explanations of the verses containing each name, and a comprehensive exposition of the multifaceted significance of these names. This is achieved through a synthesis of various branches of wisdom, as it is believed that such a harmonious integration is essential for a blissful understanding of the hidden mysteries of creation revealed in ancient scriptures. Volume 1 of this series explores the first 111 names. Subsequent volumes are planned to cover the remaining names. The selection of the initial 111 names is deliberate, as these are considered to capture the most crucial aspects and the quintessence of the entire Lalitā Sahasranāma text.*

*https://notionpress.com/in/read/lalit-priyad-pik*

## 2) Journey Through The Vēdic Thought:
## An Exploration Of Puruṣa Sūktaṃ

*Vēdic wisdom, an ancient and profound branch of knowledge, often presents a non-linear thought process that can challenge modern truth-seekers. This book aims to facilitate an understanding of the Vēdic way of thinking. It achieves this by examining the renowned Puruṣa Sūktaṃ hymn from the Rig Vēda, decoding its depths to reveal Vēdic principles. Before delving into specific Vēdic content, a foundational introduction is provided to align the reader's contemplative approach with that of the Vēdic seers. This introductory section addresses fundamental questions such as the definition of Vēda, the distinction between a Vēda and a Vēdic text, the number and significance of the Vēdās, the meaning of Chandas, the origin of Vēdic hymns, and the concept of the Vēda's eternality. Following this exploration of Vēdic foundations, the book focuses on the Puruṣa Sūktaṃ hymn itself, which comprises sixteen stanzas. Each stanza is presented with a word-by-word meaning, its import, and a detailed explanation. Diagrams are included where necessary to illustrate key concepts within the stanzas.*

*This book distinguishes itself from existing works on Puruṣa Sūkta through its unified approach and distinct goal. The approach integrates perspectives from Physics, Vēda, Upaniṣads, Esoteric studies, Occultism, Purāṇās, Etymology, and Astrology. The primary goal is not merely to interpret Puruṣa Sūktaṃ as a standalone literary work but to recognize it as a guiding light illuminating the broader Vēdic thought process. While dictionary-based interpretations of the hymns are straightforward, this book undertakes the more complex task of revealing a harmonious understanding of the hymn within the context of ancient Vēdic thought. Upon reading this book, individuals will gain a proper orientation for understanding the Vēda in the manner intended by the Vēdic seers.*

https://notionpress.com/in/read/journey-through-the-vedic-thought

## 3) The Grandeur Of Om:
## Māṇḍūkya Upaniṣad - A Meditative Approach

*Rooted in the ancient Vedic tradition passed down by enlightened seers, the utterance of any mantra is preceded by the sacred syllable "Om." The Mandukya Upanishad comprehensively addresses the profound significance of Om, exploring its essence, proper articulation, purpose, connection to our world and the divine, and practical applications in daily life.*

*This concise work elucidates these inquiries and provides practical meditative guidance for experiencing the ultimate reality. Comprising twelve aphorisms, this endeavor offers a thorough exposition of their intricacies, presenting word-for-word meanings, direct interpretations, and detailed explanations. This commentary adopts a non-traditional approach, drawing connections between various wisdom traditions, including the Vedas, Tantra, Puranas, Sri Vidya, and modern sciences. This interdisciplinary perspective aims to foster a systematic and harmonious understanding, bridging gaps in the spiritual journey of those seeking truth. Readers are invited to embark on this enigmatic exploration.*

*https://notionpress.com/in/read/the-grandeur-of-om*

**4) Suparna Suktam
(English Translation of Master E K's Telugu book)**

*Uncover the hidden treasures of Vedic knowledge with this first English translation of Master E.K.'s seminal commentary on the Suparna Sūktam. Master E.K. (Kulapati Ekkirala Krishnamacharya), a prominent spiritual teacher of the 20th century, originally wrote this insightful commentary in Telugu in 1982.*

*The Suparna Sūktam, the 164th hymn of the 1st canto of the Rig Veda, is a profound exploration of ancient wisdom, including Jyotirvidya (astronomy/astrology) and Moksha-vidya (salvation). This commentary meticulously unpacks the 52 mantras (Rks), revealing the symbolic meanings behind figures like the Suparna (Eagle-God), the Aśvam (Life Force), and the structure of the cosmos.*

*Translated with dedication by Dr. Tejaswi Katravulapally, this work makes Master E.K.'s rare and advanced insights accessible to a global audience. It is a vital resource for students of Vedic philosophy, spiritual seekers, and anyone wishing to explore the unified vision of reality presented in ancient scriptures. Prepare to be enriched with profound wisdom through this blessed offering.*

*https://worldteachertrust.org/en/web/publications/suparna-suktam*

www.ingramcontent.com/pod-product-compliance
Lightning Source LLC
Chambersburg PA
CBHW021224130726
47988CB00002B/804